SILAS MARNER

AND

MIDDLEMARCH

THOMAS A. DUFF
ASSISTANT PROFESSOR OF ENGLISH
SETON HALL UNIVERSITY

Simon & Schuster, Inc.
15 Columbus Circle
New York, NY 10023

ISBN: 0-671-00612-6

Library of Congress Catalog Card Number: 65-7246

Printed in the United States of America

CONTENTS

INTRODUCTION

SOCIAL BACKGROUND: Revolution was the key word of nineteenth century Europe. It was the age of industrial revolution, of scientific upheaval culminating in Charles Darwin's *Origin of Species,* of political transformations brought on by the appeals of nationalism, liberalism and—at length—socialism. Although it escaped the violence and bloodshed that attended the change in the continent, Britain emerged triumphant from the Napoleonic Wars, and faced a series of economic and social crises. These years, the years of maturity for George Eliot (1819-1880), and the period of the narrative in *Silas Marner,* saw indignant and ultimately successful protests against a political system which, even in its most democratic branch, the House of Commons, permitted less than one-sixth of the adult male population to exercise the franchise. A frightened autocracy fiinally acquiesced in the reform bill of 1932 which with the 1828 repeal of Test Act and the Catholic Emancipation of 1829, laid the basis for a genuine political democracy in Britain. But these measures the upper classes approved only grudgingly, while setting themselves firmly against similar reforms in economic areas. The great mass of English workers lived in appalling misery and degradation—there was much truth in Napoleon's remark that the British ruling classes treated the rabble like helots. A typical skilled textile worker received eighty shillings for a fifteen-hour, six-day week. And those that were employed were the lucky ones. Hundreds of thousands of unemployed workers lived in abject poverty in the slums of machine age cities like Birmingham and Leeds. Many of these were displaced farmers driven from their lands by the Enclosures Act. Although successful in putting English agriculture on a more efficient basis, and perhaps necessary to feed a burgeoning population, this legislation increased an already swollen labor market and aggravated the misery of the workers. Conditions in factory towns were intolerable, but the proponents of reform, such as the Scots industrialist Robert Owen or the clergyman Charles Kingsley, encountered a cold hostility from the gentry, who took comfort in the dismal dogmas of classical economists like Thomas Malthus, David Ricardo and others preaching the futility of attempting to alleviate poverty.

INTELLECTUAL AND RELIGIOUS BACKGROUND: Perhaps the strongest intellectual current of the years from 1800 to 1830 was the literary protest against the rationalism of the eighteenth century. These "romantic" writers looked back to what they considered a simpler and better era. George Eliot was quite representative of this group. Although aa German rationalist herself, she was in many ways the moral arbiter of the day. She best exemplifies the romantic novelists' concern with God, duty, responsibility, and righteousness. In her later works Eliot would come to grips with some of the social problems of the day. Occasionally she would assay a political judgment, as in her didactic novel **Felix Holt.** But in **Silas Marner** and **Adam Bede,** she has returned like many of the romantics to a pastoral and paternalistic feudal society which she innocently and inaccurately imagines England to have been in the first decades of the nineteenth century. In **Silas Marner,** the reader will not encounter rural England as it actually was in 1810, but he will find the health and plenty of a small village-like society remote from the rumblings of change. In **Middlemarch,** with its socially conscious hero and heroine, its hospital building plans, election speeches, newspaper editorials and labor distputes, the reflected mood of realism probably comes closer to depicting the real turmoil which errupted in the reign of Victoria.

LIFE: In 1857, a middle-aged English woman upon the advice of her husband assumed the pen name of George Eliot and began to publish fiction. Two of her most popular novels, *Silas Marner* and *Middlemarch,* are less widely read today, but her reputation as a major chronicler of English village life has endured for over a century. Mary Anne Evans was born in Warwickshire, England, on November 22, 1819. Her father, like Caleb Garth in *Middlemarch,* was an estate manager for several squires. He had five children, three by an earlier marriage. Mary Anne attended good boarding schools and excelled in language study until she was forced to return to supervise the family upon the death of her mother and the marriage of her sister (at which time she changed her name from Mary Anne to Marian.) Her love for language, however, did not cease; she continued her studies of German and Italian and also began the study of Hebrew. It was shortly thereafter that she renounced her Evangelical beliefs. Although she continued to respect the viewpoint of churchgoers, she remained a skeptic until her death. Her father (who had been distressed by his daughter's loss of faith) died in 1849. This was three years after Marian had published a translation of the erudite German work, *Life of Jesus (Das Leben Jesu).* She spent eighteen months living on the Continent, returning in 1851 to accept a post as assistant editor with *The Westminster Review.* Living in the London building which housed the magazine offices, she soon became immersed in a stimulating intellectual circle. It included the brilliant social philosopher Herbert Spencer, the essayist and philosopher Thomas Carlyle, and the writer and editor, George Henry Lewes. Marian's wan complexion, large, equine features and serious demeanor contrasted with the depth and acuity of her mind and the brilliance of her conversation. Lewes had a broken complexion and was extremely short, but he was witty, urbane, and a versatile writer. When they met, Lewes' wife had recently deserted him and their three children; Marian Evans and he soon formed an attachment in which she accepted the role of wife and mother, but without legal contract. The couple left immediately for a tour of Germany. Upon their return, many of their freethinking London friends accepted them, but some did not, failing to accept her action as a logical consequence of her rationalistic beliefs. The great irony for many readers of Eliot's novels is the disparity between the consistent didacticism throughout her writing and the irregularity of her relationship with Lewes.

In 1857, at the urging of Lewes, she began to publish serially her first short stories and sketches under the pseudonym George Eliot. (Notice Lewes' first name and the similarity between "Evans" and "Eliot".) The chronology of her fiction covers almost twenty years:

1857-58	*Scenes of Clerical Life* (sketches) *Amos Barton, Mr. Gilfil's Love-Story* and *Janet's Repentance* (stories)
1859	*Adam Bede*
1860	*The Mill on the Floss*
1861	*Silas Marner*
1862-63	*Romola* (published serially)
1866	*Felix Holt the Radical*
1871-72	*Middlemarch* (published serially)
1876	*Daniel Derona*

George Henry Lewes died in 1878. George Eliot died two years later, a few months after marrying John A. Cross, who was her official biographer.

CAREER: A serious and moral novelist whose chief standard for judging people was based on the extent of one's dedication to a life purpose, George Eliot's altruism is expressed in her writing goals. "My artistic purpose," she said, "is to present mixed human beings in such a way as to call forth tolerant judgment, pity and sympathy."

Her art ranges upon subjects taken from upper, middle and the lower classes of small English towns or villages. The characterizations show careful research, indicative of the worth the author placed upon industry, restraint, and conscientiousness. Gradual development of character absorbs her—and is probably her most obvious forte. Basic changes which a character undergoes are carefully plotted and explained; we observe the detailed reflective explorations of the thinking of Silas Marner, Godfrey Cass, Dorothea Brooke and Dr. Lydgate. Usually a major character is confronted with a moral choice; he lives in a responsible world in which ethical values are strong; no acts are extenuated because a person is reduced merely to responding to an environment which determines what he will choose. The failure to live wisely is ultimately punished; secret remorse, if not public censure, functions as a nemesis for foolish or evil actions. Perhaps this poetic justic is at times unduly severe: to some the fates of Dunstan Cass and John Raffles may appear capricious. To others, the sombre tone of George Eliot's homily is supposedly relieved by the warm, simple humor of lower-class talk and gossip. Reserved for tavern and clerical characters and other "acceptable" types, it is always quaint but hardly provoking.

Silas Marner and *Middlemarch* were published ten years apart. The earlier story of the weaver is a brief, well-plotted allegory about the double metamorphosis of a man. It is built on the simple change from faith to loss of faith to a regaining of faith. Eliot's debt to Wordsworth for the theme is well known: a child, more than any of the gifts offered to declining man, brings with it "hope and forward-looking thoughtts." The psychology of Silas and Godfrey Cass, the major characters, is carefully motivated and invariably credible. The scene in chapter six, at the Rainbow Tavern, has been carelessly labeled "Shakespearean," but the reader is recommended to judge for himself.

First published serially, *Middlemarch*, nearly three times as long and complex as *Silas Marner*, is considered to be George Eliot's masterpiece. Again the psychological exploration of the characters dominates the slowly moving action; here her themes include the contrast between the plans of idealists and the obstacles which life presents to hamper them; the need for compatability in mariage through unselfishness and, as in *Silas Marner*, the position of an outsider in a closely-knit society. Realistic layers of life in a nineteenth century small English town are preserved in the accurate realistic chronicle which George Eliot has recorded. After the death of Charles Dickens and the publication of *Middlemarch* George Eliot was considered to be the greatest English novelist. Surprisingly, perhaps, few have surpassed her achievement since.

DETAILED SUMMARY OF SILAS MARNER

PART ONE, CHAPTER ONE

In England during the early 1800's, men who earned a living by weaving cloth were usually looked upon with suspicion by the shepherds and peasants of the country villages. Even dogs barked at them as they went by, carrying their huge bags of raw materials. Anyone who had skill or knowledge of any kind was viewed with distrust — many villagers actually believed that weavers were under the influence of the Devil. Because people were unfriendly to them, most of the weavers lived alone and led lonely, odd lives.

> **COMMENT:** We see that the novel opens several decades after machines began to replace individual English craftsmen. We also discover that in the remote villages, weavers were thought to possess some mysterious power or skill. Because no one was friendly to them, they were forced to live alone. The effect that loneliness has upon a man is one of the primary ideas that we will see developed in the early life of Silas Marner, the weaver of Raveloe.

Silas Marner lives near the small village of Raveloe in a stone cottage situated near a deep and dangerous hole where stone had formerly been excavated. He earns his living by weaving tablecloths, fancy napkins, and other linen goods for the women of Raveloe. In his house, he has a large wooden loom which makes a soft noise as he works. Sometimes, the young boys of Raveloe peep in his window to watch him. Silas does not like to waste time; to chase them he merely opens his door to stare at them with his large, piercing eyes. The boys run in fear because, like their parents, they are afraid of the simple weaver. Silas is often asked by the villagers to help cure people with rheumatism or other illnesses; they think he surely possesses some mysterious power.

> **COMMENT:** The life that Silas Marner leads is a solitary one. He is rejected by all the people of Raveloe except when someone is ill. It is a curious fact, George Eliot observes, that at this time many country people in England did not believe in the power of God as much as they believed in the power of the Devil. People do not like Silas but they respect him because of the way he can sometimes cure sickness. Silas had no magical powers, for we learn later that he had acquired a knowledge of medicinal plants and herbs from his mother.

Situated in the middle region of England, Raveloe is far removed from the mainstream of life, it is at least an hour's ride on horseback to any of the main highways. Silas had come to this secluded spot fifteen years earlier from somewhere in Northern England. No one knew exactly where because Silas never spoke to anyone. He had always avoided the pretty girls of Raveloe and would never take time to visit the Rainbow tavern to chat with the men of the village but, once in a while, Silas became a topic for conversation. For example, once, Jem Rodney (the mole catcher) saw Silas, rigid and motionless, standing next to a fence. Jem thought Silas was dead because he didn't move at all—not even an eyelash. Jem shook him. Silas muttered "Good night" and went home. Some people thought he had a "fit" but Mr. Macey, clerk of the parish, believed that the strange conduct of the weaver was caused whenever Silas' soul left his body! Didn't Silas know a great deal about herbs? Didn't he cure Sally Oates when she was ill? Such a thing could happen to a man like Marner. It certainly could be said about him that he was odd and one further interesting fact: Silas Marner was a skillful weaver who had saved all his money for the past fifteen years. He must have a great deal of money hidden somewhere.

COMMENT: It is quite likely that the villagers in a small town like Raveioe might fail to understand why Silas Marner has strange seizures. Few people, at that time, knew very much about medicine so they did not realize that Silas suffered from catalepsy; a condition which causes a person's muscles to become rigid and his mind to go blank for a time. Silas never knew when he might get an attack nor could he remember anything that happened until after he regained consciousness. When he was much younger, Silas had two seizures of catalepsy, as we shall now see, which changed the entire course of his life.

Silas Marner was not always a lonely man. Years earlier, before he came to Raveloe, he was a young and happy man. He lived in a town in a section called Lantern Yard and was very active in a small church group in the community. One day, in church, Silas had one of his seizures at a prayer meeting. It lasted for over an hour and the members of the church, who knew Silas was a man of good example and faith, interpreted the incident as a sign of "special grace" from heaven for their fellow member. Silas' best friend was another weaver, William Dane. He was a very intelligent man who, unlike Silas, did not have a trusting, simple face. William Dane had narrow eyes and thin lips. He was always severely critical of his fellow church members or "brethren" because he said that he, at least, was positive that he was going to heaven when he died. He said the proof of this assurance of his own salvation came one day when he saw the words "calling and election (salvation) sure" mysteriously appear on the blank page of the Bible he had been reading shortly after he first joined the Lantern Yard Church Assembly. William Dane was also the only one who thought that Silas' seizure in church might have been caused by Satan (not God) entering into the soul of

Silas. Silas, however, did not mind his friend's occasional rebukes, for he was in love. Silas was engaged to be married to a beautiful girl named Sarah who worked as a servant and who loved him very much. Silas used to visit her on Sundays and, sometimes, he would even ask William Dane to join them but, shortly after the incident in the church in which he had had the cataleptic attack, Silas noted that Sarah began to act differently towards him. Her manner changed so completely (from warmth to chilliness) that Silas finally asked her if she wished to break off their engagement. Afraid because she could offer the church members no good reason, Sarah refused to end their engagement; but something happened which soon made her change her mind.

> **COMMENT:** The story of Silas is astory of change. We see now that he was not always a lonely, separated weaver. The seizure which took place in Church is interpreted as an evil sign by the person who is closest to Silas: William Dane. One can guess that the reason for the sudden change in attitude by Sarah may be because William Dane, whom we know is very critical of everyone except himself, may be influencing Sarah. In any event, we sense that something ominous is going to occur.

At this time, an elderly deacon of the church became dangerously ill and members of the community took turns caring for him day and night. Silas frequently took his turn at night; with William Dane relieving him at two o'clock in the morning. One night, when Silas was watching by the deacon's bedside, he noticed that the deacon's usually loud breathing had stopped. He was dead. Yet his death was very unusual, ofr the deacon had appeared to have regained much of his strength and everyone thought that he was on his way to recovery. Evidently the deacon had been dead for some time for his arms were rigid; it was now four o'clock in the morning. Silas wondered why William Dane had not come at two o'clock as he had expected. Silas awakened several friends, told them of the deacon's death, and then went home. At six o'clock, however, he was awakened. It was the minister of the church and William Dane. They asked Silas to come with them to the church, telling him coldly, "You shall hear." When they arrived at the prayer-meeting room, Silas found the rest of the church members waiting for them. Silas was seated in front of everyone as if he were the defendant in a trial. The minister showed him a pocket-knife and asked if it were his and where he had left it. Silas was frightened and said he did not know he had left it anywhere; the last time he remembered having it was when it was in his pocket. Then, the minister asked Silas not to hide his guilt but to confess and repent. The knife had been found in the bureau by the departed deacon's bedside. In addition, the bag of church money which was kept in the bureau was missing. The minister and the church members said the man who owned the knife was the man who stole the money. Silas was astonished. Finally, he said "God will clear me . . .

search my dwelling . . . you will find nothing but my own savings, which William Dane knows I have had these six months." The minister, however, was not changed in his opinion of Silas' guilt: "No man was with our departed brother but you, for William Dane declares to us that he was hindered by sudden sickness from going to take his place as usual." Then, the minister also accused Silas of neglecting the dead body. Silas defended himself by saying that he must have slept or that he must have had another "visitation" or seizure. He thought the thief must have entered the room and stolen the money then. Once more, he urged them to search his dwelling. The search was made and ended by William Dane's finding the empty money bag behind a chest in Silas' room! William Dane asked his friend to confess. Silas replied simply, "God will clear me." Suddenly, Silas remembered where he last had his knife. "I remember now—the knife wasn't in my pocket," but he would say no more. William Dane said he didn't know what Silas meant. "God will clear me" is all that Silas would say. The members of the community decided to find out if Silas was guilty or innocent. They prayed and then drew lots to obtain a verdict. Choosing lots is similar to picking numbers from a hat but Silas confidently hoped that God would help him and that more "non-guilty votes" would be chosen than "guilty" ones. The lots declared that Silas Marner was guilty. Silas was immediately suspended from church membership and asked to surrender the stolen money. Only if he signed a confession to show that he had repented would he be admitted back into the church. Silas refused to admit to a crime he had not committed. Turning to William Dane, he said excitedly, "The last time I remember using my knife was when I took it out to cut a strap for you!" Silas accused William Dane of the crime and, in his great sorrow over what had happened to him, he cried out, "There is no God that governs the earth righteously, but a God of lies, that bears witness against the innocent!"

Then, Silas left and thought to himself about the girl he loved, Sarah: "Soon she will leave me, too." For an entire day, he sat alone. He was too upset even to go to Sarah to make her believe in his innocence. The second day, he began to work at his loom to escape from his thoughts; a few hours had passed when the minister and a deacon came with a message from Sarah. Their engagement, she felt, was broken. Silas said nothing; he turned to work at his loom. About a month later, Sarah was married to William Dane. Shortly thereafter, the brethren in Lantern Yard learned that Silas had left the town; never to return.

COMMENT: This part of the first chapter uses a flashback to give the reasons for Silas' failure to communicate with the people with whom he lives in Raveloe. Let us attempt to determine what probably happened the night the deacon died.

(1) Silas probably had a seizure just before William Dane came

to relieve him at two o'clock. He would, therefore, be unaware of anything until he regained consciousness at four o'clock.

(2) William Dane may have suffocated the deacon for we know that he was recovering and probably did not die of natural causes.

(3) Dane probably removed the money from the drawer and then placed the knife that he had borrowed from Silas in the bureau.

(4) Dane then went to Silas' empty house, and "planted" the empty bag behind the chest in his room. He then went home and waited until the news of the deacon's death was brought to him.

(5) Arriving at the room where the deacon's death took place, Dane was the man who identified the knife as the one belonging to Silas. He then went (with the minister) to accuse Silas of the crime.

SUMMARY: The first chapter gives us the setting, in history, that we need to understand the reasons why much of the action occurs as it does. We discover that England at this time (the early nineteenth century) was primarily composed of small villages. Numerous trades still flourished before the industrial revolution, later in the century, forced many individual crafts out of business. The itinerant weaver in a community was believed to possess supernatural powers merely because he had acquired a certain skill in weaving cloth. The uneducated mind is never unwilling to imagine the impossible or to create fiction when no fact exists. So it is that Silas Marner becomes, like most outsiders in a narrow society, a social outcast. Yet, he is economically useful for he produces excellent linen goods at moderate prices; so he is, to a degree, accepted. Marner is industrious and thrifty: he flourishes and is, after fifteen years, known by all as a solitary but wealthy man.

We see that the villagers immediately mistake his catalepsy for a supernatural demon. However, they respect his knowledge of medicinal plants, a knowledge which sometimes enables him to cure illness when requested. However, the inhabitants of Raveloe know nothing of Marner's early life and disappointment. As a young man in Lantern Yard, he had been accused falsely by his friend, William Dane, of a crime he had not committed. It never occurred to the trusting Silas how foolish the church members were for choosing lots to find him guilty. Silas realized that he was merely the victim of a trap by William Dane, a trap that was based on the merest of circumstantial evidence. Yet, because he expected direct Divine intervention to prove his innocence, his simple faith was shattered when the luck of the lots went against him. He left Lantern Yard in deep despair; having lost all faith in man, woman, and God.

PART ONE, CHAPTER TWO

The great change from Lantern Yard to Raveloe can only be imagined for Silas. All the familiar scenes and faces were gone and the God he trusted in (and was disappointed by) was not prayed to by men there as in the Lantern Yard Assembly. The first thing Silas did in Raveloe was to begin working at his loom. He received an order from Mrs. Osgood and worked far into the night to finsh it earlier than she had expected.

> **COMMENT:** Picture Silas at his loom working hour after hour like a spider weaving his web. Many people find physical activity a means of escaping from boredom. Imagine how anxious Silas must have been to forget his sorrowful experiences at Lantern Yard. Every hour at the loom helped him to forget the past.

When Silas brought Mrs. Osgood her finished linen, he was paid in gold guineas. Whenever he had been paid at Lantern Yard, he gave a portion of his wages to the Church. Now the money was all his; before, he needed money for a certain purpose. Now he began to love money for itself alone. Walking home from Mrs. Osgood's in the twilight, Silas took out the money from his pocket and "thought it was brighter in the gathering gloom."

> **COMMENT:** Here is the first mention of the change in Silas towards money. He begins to lose his sense of values. Money itself becomes the chief purpose and satisfaction in his life. Because he has lost love for everything else in the "gloom" or darkness of his despair, he begins to fashion a love for hard, shiny metals: gold and silver.

Shortly after Silas arrived at Raveloe, an incident happened which made him become even more remote and separated from his neighbors in the village. One day, he gave the cobbler's ailing wife Sally Oates, some medicine he had made from foxglove (a small herb growing wild in the woods). Mrs. Oates found relief with the brown liquid mixture Silas had given her. When the other women of the village heard of the help that Sally Oates had received, they thought Silas had magical powers and they sought to have him prescribe medicines for them. Silas, however, knew he was no doctor and told all who came to him to keep their money; he would not cure them. No one believed him, though, when he said he knew no charms; everyone who had an accident or some misfortune thereafter traced its causeto Silas, saying that he probably had wished bad luck upon them.

> **COMMENT:** It is not ironic that Silas' one attempt to show kindness to another human being results only in his further separation

and loneliness?

So it was that year after year passed for Silas and the only friends he had were his gold and silver coins. Once, he broke a favorite earthenware vessel which he mended and retained as a memorial. His life was reduced to weaving at the loom and hoarding his money in an iron pot. For years, he worked sixteen hours a day and spent as little money as possible for food to keep up his strength. At night he joyfully counted his money. Silas was soon forced to keep all his gold and silver in two large, leather bags in a hole in the floor covered by bricks and sand. Each night, he would close his shutters, lock his door, brush away the sand and remove the bricks. He poured out the coins, spread them in heaps, and bathed his hands in them. He counted them and set them up in piles on the table; he felt their rounded outline with his thumb and fingers. Each coin was like a child to Silas; he would not have traded anyone of them for another. Silas had shrunk away from any thought other than his money; his heart was like a brook which had dried up into a thin, crooked crack in the earth. However, in that fifteenth year of Silas' life in Raveloe, something was about to happen during the Christmas season that was to blend his life with the lives of his neighbors.

COMMENT: Silas has become a miser. He loves the faces on his coins; not the faces of friends. He is like a prisoner in a cell who has nothing to do but to mark strokes on the wall to indicate the passage of time. Even wiser men than Silas may have devoted their lives to the unending pursuit of some goal because they have been cut off from faith and love.

SUMMARY: The second chapter shows the reasons for the complete change in Silas; from the time he first comes to Raveloe (from Lantern Yard) until fifteen years later. He seeks consolation from his grief by working long hours at his loom. His attempt to help Sally Oates with the medicinal herbs has the ultimate result of making him even lonelier. Because of his despair, he transfers his love for people to a love for money. Silas himself is slowly transformed into a hoarding miser.

PART ONE, CHAPTER THREE

In every small village there is usually one man who, because of his wealth and his family name, is more powerful than anyone else. The greatest man in Raveloe was Squire Cass. The title of Squire was given to him as a sign of respect because he was a country gentleman who owned a great deal of land. He did not work but received rent from farmers who lived on his land. England was at war with France so grain was expensive and his farmers were making great profits. Squire Cass knew they were prosperous and charged them higher rents than in peacetime. Every Christmas, many people would come to the Squire's home, the Red House. This was a large, handsome building almost directly across the street from the church. In those days, people would visit for days at a time at the holidays because travel conditions were poor and it was senseless to undergo an uncomfortable journey just for a brief visit. After the long feasting on beef and barrels of ale at the Squire's house, many people then visited Mrs. Osgood's, further up the village. The Squire's food was more abundant than Mrs. Osgood's but hers was better prepared. This was because the Squires' wife had died and there was no woman living at the Red House to add the feminine touch.

COMMENT: This chapter introduces the second plot in the novel; the story of the Squire's son, Godfrey Cass. Later, we shall see how the action of this plot intersects with the action in the story of Silas Marner. Notice that the Squire's income is dependent upon the rent he collects from his tenant farmers; and that the custom of the prosperous land owner was to entertain for prolonged periods at the holidays throughout the year. Recall that the author indicated that something important was going to happen to Silas Marner during the Christmas season.

The Squire had several sons who did not work because he permitted them to be idle like himself. Godfrey Cass was the eldest. He was a friendly, good-natured and handsome young man who was first in line to inherit his father's land. His younger brother Dunstan or "Dunsey," as he was called, was a thick-set, heavy looking and mean kind of man who spent most of his time drinking or gambling. Most people in the village did not like Dunsey; nor did they particularly care what happened to him. They were concerned, however, that Godfrey, whom everyone liked, seemed to be going down the same road as Dunsey. Godfrey had been away from home for days at a time. It looked, for a while, as if he were going to marry the pretty Nancy Lammeter. She was Mrs. Osgood's niece (Nancy's mother had died) who came to live at the Red House. However, she had heard about Godfrey's recent conduct and, if Godfrey failed to turn over a new leaf, he might lose her.

COMMENT: Our first reaction is to favor Godfrey over Dunsey. Our decision is based on the quality of the person's character and, here, the difference between the two brothers is obvious. We also learn of the romantic bond which exists between Nancy Lammeter and Godfrey. Our curiosity is provoked when we learn that Godfrey has often been absent from the Red House for long periods of time. In the next scene, we discover why.

It is late November in that fifteenth year of Silas Marner's life at Raveloe. The setting is a parlour of the Red House. It is late afternoon and the fading light is shining on Godfrey Cass who stands before the fire with an angry look on his face. The door opens; it is Dunsey. His face is flushed from excessive drinking. Angrily, Godfrey tells him that he must hand over the one hundred pounds rent from Fowler (a farmer) to the Squire; or else admit that he gave it to Dunsey. The Squire, it seems, is threatening to seize Fowler's goods if the rent is not paid within a week. Dunsey refuses flatly to pay back the rent money he has borrowed from Godfrey saying, "You'll not refuse me the kindness to pay it back for me. I might tell the Squire how his handsome son was married to that nice young woman, Molly Farren, and was very unhappy because he couldn't live with his drunken wife." Godfrey seizes Dunsey by the arm and excitedly insists, "I have no money: I can get no money." Godfrey had borrowed money from a man named Kimble but he would not lend Godfrey any more. Dunstan suggests that Godfrey sell his beautiful horse, Wildfire, at the hunt the next morning but Godfrey is planning to go to a party at Mrs. Osgood's house the next night and does not wish to return home late and dirty from the hunt. Dunsey begins to tease Godfrey about the party and Nancy Lammeter; "And there's sweet Miss Nancy coming; and we shall dance with her, and promise never to be naughty again, and be taken into favour, and —" Godfrey turns red with anger. Dunsey sits in a chair and begins to tap the end of his whip in the palm of his hand. He reminds Godfrey that his secret wife, Molly Farren, is also a drug addict. Next he hints at an evil solution to Godfrey's problem (about being unable to marry Nancy since he already has a wife) by wondering what might happen ". . . if Molly should happen to take a drop of laudanum (a liquid made from opium) some day, and make a widower of you. Nancy wouldn't mind being a second, if she didn't know it." Godfrey becomes pale. He wonders if he should tell the Squire everything. He knows that Molly Farren may tell of their marriage because he has not enough money for her. "You drain me of money till I have got nothing to pacify her with, and she'll do as she threatens some day. It's all one. I'll tell my father everything myself, and you may go to the devil." Finally, Godfrey agrees to let Dunsey ride his horse to the hunt the next morning to sell him. However, he warns him to be careful not to drink for he might seriously injure himself or Wildfire. Dunsey laughs confidently and then leaves.

COMMENT: This is one of the most important scenes in the novel, so far, because it presents the background on the chief problems that Godfrey Cass must attempt to solve. Dunsey Cass is blackmailing his brother. He knows that Godfrey entered into a degrading marriage with Molly Farren; a woman whose weaknesses were both alcoholic and narcotic. It was an ugly story of low passion that the author does not fully explain except to tell us that the marriage was a trap laid by Dunstan's cunning so that he could satisfy his jealous hate of Godfrey and obtain blackmail money from him. Godfrey has several things to worry about:

(1) He has given the rent money from Fowler to Dunstan and

now must sell his horse, Wildfire, to get enough cash to pay the Squire.

(2) The Squire may find out about his marriage and turn him out of the house in disgrace.

(3) If Nancy Lammeter learns his secret she will refuse to see him. Although he cannot ask her to marry him because of his marriage, he does love her and enjoys her companionship above anything else.

After Dunsey left, Godfrey was alone with his thoughts. He thought of the four years he had courted Nancy; of how he could have changed his idle habits and become a good husband to her. Now, however, that was impossible, and his situation would be worse if his ugly secret was discovered. Both his father and Nancy would turn their backs on him then. He would lose both his inheritance and the one woman who could have changed his life for the better. Godfrey, wishing to escape his bitter thoughts, decides to spend another idle evening at the Rainbow tavern.

COMMENT: We have seen how Silas Marner changed; now we see that another good-humored, affectionate person can become hate-filled towards life when he thinks of the sorrow his own wrong-doing has caused. Silas was the victim of chance and the evil of others; Godfrey was guilty of willfully committing an act but he was, also, the victim of his brother's disgraceful plotting.

PART ONE, CHAPTER FOUR

The next morning, Dunstan Cass sets out to sell Wildfire at the hunt. It is a wet, foggy day and, when he passes the cottage of Silas Marner, he notices that the deserted stone pit is filled to the brim with red, muddy water. He hears Silas' loom through the mist and suddenly thinks of frightening the old weaver into giving him money to pay the debts he owes. Then, he decides that he will receive enough money from the sale of Wildfire to satisfy Godfrey so he continues on his way. At Batherley, he sells the horse to a man named Bryce for one hundred and twenty pounds; the money to be paid only after Wildfire is delivered safe and sound to the Bryce stables. However, Dunsey, foolishly drinking and swaggering, then decides to ride Wildfire in the hunt. Unfortunately, the horse is soon killed, pierced by a sharp stake when it fails to clear a fence in a jump. Dunsey had exhausted its energy by forcing it to jump excessively. Now that Wildfire is dead, there will be no money to give to Godfrey. Dunstan is uninjured; he swears, takes another drink, and begins walking back to Raveloe . . . swishing the riding whip he had taken from Godfrey that morning. The name Godfrey Cass was cut in deep letters on the golden handle. (This is an important fact to remember for the whip is discovered much later in the story.) The road is covered with fog and the falling rain makes the ground slippery. Suddenly, seeing a light coming from Silas Marner's cottage, Dunstan thinks of borrowing money from him. After receiving no answer to his knock, Dunstan is surprised to find that the door is unlocked and the cottage empty. Silas has gone on a short errand. A piece of meat tied with string and fastened at the other end to Silas' huge door key is dangling near the fire roasting slowly. Silas never bought very much meat because it was expensive, and he did not buy the proper utensils with which to cook it in his fireplace. This piece of pork was a gift from Priscilla Lammeter, Nancy's sister. Because he used to hang his door key on a pot hanger suspended above the fire, he could not lock his door when he left to go to the village to purchase some twine for his loom. Dunstan knows that Marner probably keeps his money in his cottage. Why not steal the money? Searching the room, Dunstan Cass brushes away the sand, removes the bricks in the floor, and lifts out the two heavy bags of gold hidden in the hole. He then replaces the bricks and sand, and leaves, closing the door behind him carefully. Dunsey, holding the whip and the heavy gold, begins to step away through the darkness and the mist.

COMMENT: The theft of the weaver's gold is an action which joins the plot of Silas Marner with the plot of Godfrey Cass. Notice how the author skillfully plans the circumstances leading up to the reasons why Dunstan would be at the cottage of Silas and why Silas would be absent. Silas did not want to waste time, the following morning, away from his loom, so he went to Raveloe that night for twenty minutes while his food was being cooked. Even the reason for the door's being open when Dunstan arrived is logically explained by the use which Silas made of the door key.

PART ONE, CHAPTER FIVE

Silas returns home just a few minutes after Dunstan Cass has left. He never dreamed that any thief would steal from him, and, for fifteen years, no one had even attempted to do so. Entering his cottage, he scuffs over the footprints Dunstan had left in the sand, puts down his lantern, and the sack with the twine, and resumes his preparation for dinner. Wishing to count his gold while eating his dinner, Silas sweeps away the sand without perceiving any change and removes the bricks. Gone! His hand trembles. Again and again, he looks; he searches the entire house . . . in vain. Finally, he sits down at his loom and begins to wonder: Was it a thief or some "unseen power" that stole his money? Silas thinks and thinks; at last, he decides that the man who robbed him must be Jem Rodney.

COMMENT: Silas believes Jem is the thief for three reasons:

(1) Jem was known to be a poacher; that is, he trespassed illegally on other people's land to hunt game.

(2) Once Jem had made a jesting remark to Silas about his money.

(3) Jem had come in to light his pipe at Silas' fire one night and lingered there instead of leaving immediately.

To catch the thief, Silas knows he needs help from the people of the village. He runs out into the rain to the Rainbow tavern where he knows the men of the town often gathered in the evening.

PART ONE, CHAPTER SIX

This chapter is viewed by some as one of the finest chapters in English literature because of the outstanding picture of small village characters (and their conversation) which George Eliot has drawn for us. The scene is in the kitchen of the Rainbow tavern where the less prosperous men of the village sit, smoke, and talk. The butcher is questioned about a Durham cow he says he has purchased from Mr. Lammeter. However, the farrier (cow veterinary) tells the butcher that he knows that the cow was drenched (given medicine for sickness). The landlord of the Rainbow, Mr. Snell, is the peacemaker when disputes arise; he changes the subject. Mr. Macey, the elderly clerk, and Ben Winthrop, the wheel maker, tease Mr. Tookey, the worried little deputy-clerk, about his poor singing voice and his ambition to better himself. Again, the landlord changes the subject by asking Mr. Macey about his brother Solomon, who plays the fiddle. This question soon prompts Mr. Macey to tell a long narrative about how the first Mr. Lammeter came to Raveloe years before and about the marriage of his son, the present Mr. Lammeter. The others in the Rainbow have heard Mr. Macey's stories many times but they love to hear them again. Mr. Macey then retells the history of the Warrens, the Lammeter estate, and of Mr. Cliff, the mad tailor from "Lunnon" (London) who used to own it.

The Lammeter stables are still called "Cliff's Holiday" and are, supposedly, inhabited by ghosts. Mr. Dowlas, the cow doctor, scoffing at such an idea, is willing to wager that no ghosts are in the stables. However, the landlord and, especially, Mr. Macey believe in ghosts and consider someone who does not to be ignorant.

COMMENT: Notice that no action in the novel occurs in this chapter. Rather, we have a warm, humorous scene described with realistic dialogue and marked insight into character. Contrast this chapter with the previous one's gloomy and depressing tone.

The fact that the men are discussing ghosts is deliberately planned to make the entrance of Silas more effective dramatically.

PART ONE, CHAPTER SEVEN

Just then, Silas Marner enters the room silently. He is dripping wet and staring with his large, strange eyes. The men are startled and jerk their long pipes like insects waving their antennae. Silas does have an unearthly, ghostly appearance. The landlord is the first to speak to Silas: "What's your business?" Silas can utter only: "Robbed! I've been robbed." He demands that he be taken to the constable or to Squire Cass or Mr. Crackenthorp. The Landlord thinks Silas is mad and tells Jem Rodney, who is closest to the weaver, to seize him. Jem, however, refuses and seizes his drinking can when Silas asks him if he stole the money. Silas is forced to sit and tell his story from the beginning.

COMMENT: The unusual situation in which Silas finds himself is that he is now mixing among his fellow men. He needs their help and they are interested in his problem. This scene marks the beginning of the stirring of feeling inside Silas for his neighbors... for the first time in fifteen years.

Most of the men who listen sympathetically to the account of the robbery believe that the devil is probably the one who has stolen the money. They have difficulty, however, trying to estimate why the devil waited until the door was unlocked before attempting to take it. The landlord defends Jem Rodney and is supported by Mr. Macey. They tell Silas that Jem has been with them in the tavern. Silas approaches Jem says, "I was wrong," admitting that Jem was the first person he had thought of as the robber; because he had been in Silas' home more than anyone else.

COMMENT: Jem Rodney is freed of suspicion of the robbery. Once more, Silas is forced to come to think about others; in his sorrow for accusing Jed, he shows pity for him, also.

Silas tells the farrier he has lost two hundred and seventy-two pounds of money (which, by today's standards, would be the equivalent of a fortune). The farrier suggests that Silas go with two of the "sensibilest" men of the group to the constable, Master Kench. The farrier knows the constable is ill and he is hoping to be appointed deputy. However, Mr. Macey intervenes and says that the law "forbids" cow doctors to be deputies. The farrier objects and disagrees with a law which would prevent him from receiving the honor of deputy. The landlord, as usual, makes peace and Mr. Dowlas (the farrier) and another man leave with Silas who must once again go out into the rain.

COMMENT: It is significant to observe that the townspeople themselves, as well as Silas, are beginning to soften their hearts.

PART ONE, CHAPTER EIGHT

The next morning, the entire village is excited with the news of the robbery. The rain has washed away all footprints at the stone pits but a tinder-box (a small box which holds kindle and which is ignited by sparks from striking flint rock with steel) is found, in the mud, in the vicinity. It is not Silas' box, although some suspicious people think it is. Mr. Macey does not believe the tinder box is a clue because he still argues that spirits have made off with the money. Mr. Crackenthorp (the rector of the church), Squire Cass, and other men of importance think that the tinder-box may belong to a dark-skinned peddler, who had recently been in Raveloe selling his trinkets and wares. Mr. Crackenthorp is curious: "Did he wear earrings?" Mr. Snell gives an evasive answer, trying to say "yes" and "no" at the same time. Others are questioned and, eventually, it is decided that the peddler did wear earrings.

COMMENT: Here George Eliot gives us further insight into the life of a small community of this period. We perceive that the robbery has the effect of making the comparatively dull members of the community suddenly become excitable. Observe how each is ready to believe the wildest interpretation without having the facts necessary for proof. The passage about the earrings is especially humorous because the truth of whether the peddler wore them or not makes no difference in his guilt or innocence.

Silas is questioned about the peddler but he says that he did not permit him to enter his house. Silas is hoping that the peddler might be the culprit and he can readily picture his gold in the peddler's box. The people in the village think the peddler is guilty and are not ready to believe Silas because:

(1) Silas has poor eyesight from the close work he has done at his loom over the years. He would not see a man prowling near his house as other men would.

(2) Some people believe that Silas is a half-crazy miser and that his testimony about the peddler cannot be believed.

(3) Men who wear rings are known to be criminals sometimes. The villagers assume erroneously, therefore, that the peddler (whom they *think* wears earrings) is the thief.

Godfrey Cass, meanwhile, had returned from Mrs. Osgood's party and had gone to bed without worrying about Dunstan because he realized that, perhaps, Dunstan had to wait a day to sell Wildfire. Another possibility was that he may have slept in Batherley at the Red Lion Inn instead of coming home in the fog. Down at the Rainbow, the next day, he meets Mr. Snell and tells him he thought the peddler a "merry, grinning fellow" and it is all nonsense about his evil looks. Some think Godfrey will go to the town of Tarley to find the peddler to prove Mr. Snell is wrong. Godfrey, however, mounts his horse and heads, not toward Tarley, but toward Batherley. Hoping to find Dunstan and annoyed with himself for trusting his horse to him, he rides until he finally meets Bryce, who tells him that the body of Wildfire has been found. Godfrey conceals his great fear and leaves. On the way back to Raveloe, Godfrey debates about telling his father that he gave the Fowler's rent money to Dunstan. He knows he has done wrong by giving the money to his worthless brother but he does not wish his father to think he spent it on himself: "I'd never have spent the money for my own pleasure," he muses, "I was tortured into it." Godfrey thinks his father may not be so severe with him if he explains how Dunstan blackmailed him for the money. He may also tell his father about his secret marriage; perhaps, the Squire would prefer to keep the marriage a secret to protect his own pride. Godfrey knew his father has a careless habit of permitting situations to worsen and suddenly taking severe measures to correct them. For example, the Squire often permitted his tenant farmers to neglect their fences, fail to pay their rent, and, in general, to manage their farms poorly; but, when he needed money, he was extremely demanding with them and would not listen to any appeal. With these thoughts, Godfrey goes to bed, promising himself to tell the Squire everything the next morning. However, when he awakes, all he can think of are the consequences:

(1) His disgrace with his father.
(2) His complete and final loss of Nancy Lammeter.

Godfrey changes his mind again. He will not tell his father; perhaps, Dunstan will return in a few days with money and all will be well.

COMMENT: In this chapter, we witness the hopelessness of the vilagesr in attempting to solve the theft of Marner's gold: much of their debating and theorizing is amusing, especially that part of it which attempts to fix the blame upon the peddler. We see how irrelevant their approach is to the evidence. For example, when they spend time determining if the peddler wore earrings or not, they are merely quarreling among themselves. The second string of the plot in this chapter belongs to Godfrey. We see his disappointment upon discovering that Wildfire has been killed, and we wonder if he is going to tell all to his father. However, as the chapter ends, we find that Godfrey's chief weaknesses (indecision and timidity) are still with him. He lives on in his world of appearance; both his father and Nancy are deceived but, to tell them the truth, means to shatter his own happiness. This act Godfrey is unable to do.

PART ONE, CHAPTER NINE

The chapter begins with a description of Squire Cass, before breakfast, on the morning that Godfrey is to speak with him about the rent money which he gave to Dunstan. About sixty years of age, Godfrey's father is tall and stout. He has a knitted brow but a "slack, feeble mouth." He is careless in his personal habits; his dress is slovenly. Yet, he has no superior in the village; so, he speaks with great authority. He views everything he owns as the oldest and the best. Godfrey approaches him at the table and tells him, first, that Wildfire was injured; finally, he admits that Dunsey has killed the horse. He also reveals that he has lent Fowler's rent to his brother. The Squire becomes purple with anger. He reminds Godfrey that he is not required, by law, to leave his money or lands to Godfrey when he dies. He wishes to speak with Dunsey, fearing some kind of trick is being attempted, "and you've been bribing him not to tell."

COMMENT: Imagine how frightened Godfrey is when his father suggests that there may be something hidden which Godfrey does not reveal. The dramatic value in the scene resides in the reader's knowledge; knowledge that a character (the Squire) does not possess.

The Squire is determined to disown Dunstan, "to turn him out without a cent." He tells Godfrey that he is disappointed with his conduct, especially in light of the possible marriage he had anticipated between Godfrey and Nancy Lammeter. He asks Godfrey if, perhaps, she had refused his marriage proposal. Godfrey admits that she hasn't but he does not think she will accept. The Squire laughs at this comment, expressing an opinion that Nancy's father would not be unwilling to have his daughter marry into the family. He tells Godfrey to ask her to marry him now; if Godfrey refuses, he shall disown him. He ends by telling Godfrey to sell Dunsey's horse for the money because he will not permit him to live at the Red House any longer. The Squire says, "He shan't hang on me any more."

COMMENT: Godfrey has both freed himself and made his chains stronger. On the one hand, he has told his father two important truths:
(1) He has given the one hundred pounds' rent money to Dunstan.
(2) Dunstan has killed Wildfire, Godfrey's valuable horse.

In both instances, Godfrey has fared much better than he had expected. His father scolds him for being foolish enough to lend both the rent and, later, the horse to Dunsey. He decides to turn Dunsey out of the house, forever; yet, on the other hand, Godfrey has made his trouble worse:

(1) His father demands that he ask Nancy to marry him or he will disown him, too.

(2) He cannot marry Nancy, even if she consents, because of his secret marriage to Molly Farren. He would be forced to refuse her if she did wish to marry him.

Godfrey is unrealistic. The chapter ends with his choosing to leave things alone; in the hope that chance will resolve his difficulties. Similarly, the author adds, many men spend more than they earn, neglect their responsibilities, betray friendships and secrets, and attempt ambitions beyond their power in the belief that chance will create success. The one thing such people pray against is the one thing they can be certain of: that a certain seed bears a certain fruit. In other words, chance cannot change that which is certain to happen.

PART ONE, CHAPTER TEN

Justice Malan of Tarley, a magistrate, supervises the investigation of the robbery of Silas Marner's money. The chief suspect is the peddler and a lengthy description of him: "curly black hair," "wearing large rings," and so forth is spread throughout the countryside. Many peddlers, however, fit this description so it is impossible to trace the blame to a single one. Weeks pass and people soon lose interest in the case. Excitement has died down in Ravloe, also. No one even misses Dunstan Cass who has not been seen since the day he killed Wildfire, Godfrey's horse. Once before, Dunstan had been gone from home for a long period of time. The villagers of Raveloe do not suspect Dunstan of the robbery even though he disappeared on the same day that Marner's money was stolen.

COMMENT: It is logical that Dunstan is not suspected as the thief:

(1) The Cass family, with its proud ancestry and wealth, would not ordinarily be associated with any crime whatsoever. People in Raveloe hesitate to suggest evil of reputable families.

(2) Christmas time is coming and the gaiety of the season, with its abundance of puddings and drink, dulls the minds of many people.

Down at the Rainbow tavern, the opinion of the robbery is divided into two viewpoints:

(1) Some feel that there is a logical explanation for the loss of the money. They maintain that the clue of the tinder box fixes the blame upon the peddler.
(2) Others suggest that the only way to view the robbery is as a supernatural mystery which can never be solved.

Silas Marner himself feels a profound sense of loss because his money has been stolen. To other people, his life has been withered and shrunken (as it was) but, to Silas, it has been an eager life. The money has been the one thing he could cling to; it is the only thing that has satisfied him. Now, it is gone. Silas still has his loom and his work, of course, but the prospect of counting his money each night is over. He can receive no delight from the new money he makes for it only reminds him of how much he has lost. He fills up his unhappy life by weaving; at night, now that he cannot count his money, he sits by his fire, leans his elbows on his knees, clasps his head with his hands, and moans softly.

> **COMMENT:** The love that Silas had for people was lost years ago at Lantern Yard when he was accused falsely of stealing money. At Raveloe, he had created a new love; for money. The stealing of his gold, however, leaves him with nothing to love. Notice how Eliot has paralleled the early life of Silas with his current experience. In both instances, a robbery was instrumental in causing Silas' great sorrow.

The villagers in Raveloe begin to show affection and charity towards Silas. Mrs. Osgood sends him various gifts of food; as do other people who have made extra puddings and roasts for the Christmas season. Mr. Crackenthorp, the rector at the church, gives Silas some pigs' feet. Many people stop in at Silas' cottage to ask him to repeat the details of the robbery; or to try to cheer him.

Mr. Macey, the village clerk, visits Silas and gives him a long talk; advising him not to sit moaning about his money. He asks Silas if he has a Sunday suit because he is anxious to have Silas attend weekly services at Church. Silas replies that he does not own such a suit. Mr. Macey promises then to have his assistant, Mr. Tookey, make a suit at a low price so that Silas may come to Church and "be a bit neighborly." Silas is unsure, though, about going to church for he has not gone in fifteen years. Mr. Macey leaves, thinking Silas is so "muddled" that he probably does not even know when Sunday comes around each week.

Another person who comes to comfort Silas is Mrs. Dolly Winthrop, wife of the wheelmaker, Ben Winthrop. She is a kind, patient woman who seeks out the sadder and more serious things in life so that she can be of help. She always seems to find time to visit some one who is ill or needs her assistance. The good, wholesome woman is aware of the suffering of Silas and, one Sunday afternoon, she visits him; taking her little seven-year-old boy, Aaaron, with her. Dolly has baked lard cakes for Silas but she cannot read the lettering on them. Aaron is shy and hides behind one of Silas' chairs. Silas reads the lettering; it is "I.H.S." (initials representing the name of Christ.) He then thanks Dolly for bringing the cakes. Dolly wishes to have Silas begin to attend church and she speaks to him; trying to persuade him. Silas tells her that he has never been to a Raveloe church but that he had belonged to a small chapel (Lantern Yard) years ago. Again Dolly, recommends that Silas go to church. Aaron asks for another cake and, soon, Dolly makes him sing for Silas. Aaron sings "God rest you, merry gentlemen." Silas thanks him but he has not been listening carefully at all. Mrs. Winthrop and Aaron leave after she makes one final attempt to win Silas to churchgoing.

Notwithstanding the attempts of Mr. Macey and Dolly Winthrop, Silas spends his Christmas day alone. No one could ever suspect that he was once a man who loved others with tenderness.

Every Christmas, Doctor Kimble (who loved to recall his early experiences as a doctor) and his wife came to the home of Squire Cass to drink spirits and to play cards. The great celebration at the Red House, however, was not on Christmas but on New Year's Eve. Every year, the Squire held a dance and all the society of Raveloe and Tarley came and stayed for several days. Godfrey was looking forward to the long, happy days of the New Year's Eve celebration but, in his mind, he could hear the voice of Anxiety whispering to him that Dunsey might come home; that more money might be needed (Godfrey would have to sell his dead mother's diamond pin) and that Squire Cass might attempt to bring Nancy and Godfrey into a marriage match which Godfrey could only decline. Then, Godfrey thought only of looking into Nancy's eyes. He joined the noisy Christmas company and did much drinking; yet, even then, he could still hear the voice of Anxiety.

SUMMARY: In this chapter we discover:

(1) The people soon forget about the robbery of Silas' gold; they assume that the peddler is guilty.

(2) No one suspects Dunstan Cass of the robbery.

(3) Silas is deep in sorrow and gloom after his loss; although the townspeople begin to show greater fondness and charity towards him, he seems unable to respond. Both Mr. Macey and Dolly Winthrop are unsuccessful in their attempts to interest Silas in church.

(4) Godfrey's situation has not changed. He looks forward to the

New Year's Eve dance for the happiness it will bring. He pushes out of his mind, as best he can, thoughts of his problems or of the future.

PART ONE, CHAPTER ELEVEN

Nancy Lammeter arrives at the Red House for the long festivities of New Year's; she rides (sitting side-saddle) on a little pillow . . . on the same horse as her Father. Godfrey helps her down and she enters the house to be greeted by Mrs. Kimble (the doctor's wife and the sister of Squire Cass). She goes upstairs to the Blue Room where her clothes boxes had been sent; here, the other ladies are grooming themselves for a before-dinner tea. In the room, Nancy sees six young ladies; including a pair of unattractive sisters from the city of Lytherly. The two Miss Gunns are dressed in the height of fashion; perhaps even beyond good taste. Nancy talks to Mrs. Osgood (her aunt) exchanging pleasant greetings. Mrs. Osgood likes Nancy very much and has given her some family jewelry as presents even though Nancy has refused to marry Gilbert Osgood because he is a cousin. (Nancy's dead mother and Mrs. Osgood were sisters.) Three of the ladies leave the room but the Gunn sisters remain; curious to see what kind of gown a country girl like Nancy might have. Nancy unpacks her boxes; revealing her beautiful, costly, and well-kept clothes. The Gunn sisters notice privately that Nancy is truly a lady in her dress and manners. Only her hands are not aspretty as they might otherwise be because she performs many chores at home. Also, Nancy mispronounces certain words saying, for example, "mate" for "meat" and "oss" for "horse."

Nancy's sister, Priscilla Lammeter, bursts into the room. She is five years older than Nancy and lacks the beauty and grace of her younger sister. Priscilla is a frank, talkative, tactless person who will say what she thinks; regardless of what others may think. She knows she has a ruddy complexion, and is not, perhaps, very attractive to men but she does not care about men anyway. She prefers to remain single and to be independent; saying, "Mr. Have-Your-Own-Way is the best husband." Priscilla wears the same color dress that Nancy wears because Nancy wishes them to look like sisters. Priscilla knows she will not appear as pretty even when the dress is just as pretty. "For I am ugly," she says; then, turning to the Gunn sisters, she adds, "But, law! I don't mind, do you?"

Nancy and Priscilla descend the stairs and enter the parlour. Mr. Crackenthorp, the rector, makes a playful remark to Nancy about Godfrey after Godfrey leads her to a seat next to him. Squire Cass is in a jovial mood and speaks to the rector and Mrs. Crackenthorp (a small, mousy type of woman) about Nancy's great beauty. Mr. Lammeter hears the compliment but does not let it appear that he is gratified or elated at the possibilities of a marriage between his daughter and Godfrey; not unless there is an alteration in Godfrey's conduct will he give his consent.

Doctor Kimble, his wife, the Squire, and Priscilla Lammeter have a conversation about Priscilla's cooking and Mrs. Kimble's. Dr. Kimble complains laughingly that his wife puts black pepper in his food whenever he offends her. He calls it "an awful tit-for-tat."

> **COMMENT:** We are shown realistic scenes like this one throughout the book. Recall the pleasant recording of country conversation heard in the scene at the Rainbow Tavern. It is characteristic of the skill of George Eliot that she can capture the mood of gaiety in a few lines, transmitting it to the reader in authentic, idiomatic nineteenth century speech.

Solomon Macey is an old, white-haired man whom the Squire asks to play the fiddle for the company. The chairs are pushed back and everyone follows him into the White Parlour (where the mistletoe and holly are hung) to begin the dance. The Squire leads the dance with Mrs. Crackenthorp; joining hands with the Rector and Mrs. Osgood. Mr. Macey watches them as they dance. He observes that the Squire is rather spry "considering his weight" and that the rector "might do worse, he might do worse." Ben Winthrop, the husband of Dolly, is there with Aaron; watching and also making comments. Aaron wishes to know if one of the feathers in a woman's hat is actually sticking out of her head! Nancy and Godfrey are dancing; Ben remarks that Nancy is a lovely girl. Mr. Macey is critical of Godfrey for permitting himself to be influenced by Dunsey and for letting him have Wildfire, for this resulted in the death of the horse. Both he and Ben wonder if the young couple will eventually be united in marriage.

Nancy and Godfrey suddenly leave the dance floor because Squire Cass has stepped on the train of Nancy's dress. Priscilla hurries to fetch thread and needle as Godfrey and Nancy wait in a small parlour adjoining the dance. Nancy is sorry for causing trouble but Godfrey tells her that one dance with her means more to him than any other pleasure in the world. Nancy disagrees because of Godfrey's past action towards her. She admits she would like to see a change in him but she refuses to encourage him. Godfrey accuses her of having no feeling for him but she replies, "I think those have the least feeling that act wrong to begin with." A quarrel is about to ensue but Priscilla enters. Boldly, Godfrey asks Nancy if she wants him to leave. Nancy leaves the decision to him. Godfrey, determined to get as much joy as possible out of each moment because he fears the future, answers, "Then I like to stay."

SUMMARY: The chapter opens with Nancy's arrival at the Red House for the beginning of the New Year's festivities. We notice:

(1) The expected custom, in rural England at the holiday season, was to have lavish expenditures of food and drink presented by the chief men of prominence and wealth in the community.

(2) Nancy Lammeter is a refined woman of taste and manner although she has not received a full education.

(3) Priscilla Lammeter is a foil, or mirror, for her sister. She represents the unsophisticated, realistic kind of woman one might expect to find in a community far removed from cultural advantages; yet, we like her much more than the Gunn sisters who, for all their knowledge of fashion and education, lack the basic human warmth of Priscilla and her sister.

(4) The social aspects of English life in this period are captured in the description and conversation of numerous secondary characters such as Dr. Kimble, his wife, Ben Winthrop, the Rector, Mr. Macey, and his brother, Solomon Macey, the fiddler.

(5) Nancy is decidedly interested in Godfrey, but Godfrey's situation remains unchanged. He loves her but he cannot marry her because he is secretly married to Molly Farren; a woman addicted to alcohol and drugs.

PART ONE, CHAPTER TWELVE

While Godfrey was speaking to Nancy Lammeter, his wife (Molly Farren) was walking in the snow to Raveloe carrying her child in her arms. She was dressed in rags and shivered with each step. Her purpose was to go to the Red House to reveal that she was Godfrey's wife. She wished to disgrace him for he had said that he would sooner die than admit that she was his wife. Godfrey had given her enough money on which to live but she had always spent it on opium (at this time there were no laws against its scale). Molly had set out at an early hour but had lingered; hoping the snow would stop. Now, it was seven o'clock and the snow was deep. She had a bottle of Laudanum (liquid opium) and took a drink. Emptying it, she threw the bottle away. Soon, however, she became drowsy and wanted to sleep. Still clutching the child tightly in her arms, she lay down on a small furze bush in the snow to sleep. The drink had numbed her senses; she could not feel the cold of the snow nor the freezing wind. Soon, her fingers lost their tension and the child cried, "Mammy," but the mother's ear was deaf to any sound.

The child rolled from the mother and began walking in the snow towards a bright light from a cottage. The light came from the fire of Silas Marner's cottage. Slowly, the child made its way through the snow until it reached the door and the door was wide open! Walking directly to the warm fireplace, the child sat down before the fire; happy and contented. Soon she fell asleep.

And where was Silas Marner when this small visitor arrived? He was in the cottage but he did not see the child. Since the robbery, Marner had developed the habit of opening his door several times each night and looking out to see if someone might be coming to his house with the lost gold. Some of the villagers had told him that he should sit up on New Year's Eve to welcome the new year because it might bring him good luck. Several times, he had opened the door and had looked to see if anyone were coming. Once a dark figure (Molly Farren) could actually be seen walking through the snow, but Silas did not see her for he had suddenly been seized with a cataleptic attack. He stood there, rigid and motionless, with his right hand on the open door and did not see the child enter his home.

COMMENT: We see why the door is open when the child approaches the cottage. Silas is still susceptible to the seizures and one occurs when he has opened the door hoping to see someone returning with his gold.

When his senses finally return, Silas turns to fix the logs in his fire; suddenly, he thinks he sees his gold before the hearth! He reaches out to touch it but he feels warm curls rather than the hard outline of his coins. Amazed, Silas kneels; bending his head to examine the beautiful little girl. At first, he thinks the child may be his little sister, Hephzibah, who died when he was a small boy. Or is it a dream? Silas has not realized that the child entered when he had the seizure at the open door. Silas picks up the child, feeds her porridge with brown sugar, and removes her wet boots. He realizes that she must have been walking in the snow in order to have wet her feet. Picking up the child, he opens his door and follows the small footprints which she had made in the snow. The child soon cries, "Mammy," and Silas is then aware that in the bush before him is a snow-covered body.

SUMMARY: In this chapter, we witness the attempt by Godfrey's wife, Molly Farren, to revenge herself upon him. She drinks the laudanum, however, and dies in the snow. Her blond-haired baby girl, Godfrey's child, manages to escape a similar fate by entering Silas Marner's cottage and warming herself at the fire. The door is open because:

(1) Silas is hoping to see someone coming to return his stolen money.
(2) He is seized by a cataleptic attack and remains perfectly rigid until after the child has entered his house.

Observe the parallel between the loss of Silas' gold and the discovery of the golden-haired girl. Both incidents occur at night; once, the fog obscured Dunstan; now, the snow has concealed the approach of Molly Farren. In both instances, the door of Marner's cottage is open. He has had two strange occurrences in two months: in the first, he loses his golden coins; in the second, he finds a golden child.

PART ONE, CHAPTER THIRTEEN

At the Red House, the party is in full pitch: the Squire is talking loudly, Dr. Kimble is absorbed in a game of cards, and the servants have come up from the kitchen to peek in at the dancers in the White Parlour. Squire Cass is praising his young son Bob for his dancing ability; Godfrey has his eyes on Nancy Lammeter. Just after Godfrey lifts his eyes away from glancing at her, he sees his own child being carried in the arms of Silas Marner! Silas has come through the door at the other end of the room. The Squire and the Rector ask Silas what is the matter; Silas tells them he has come for a doctor. The Rector wishes to know why the doctor is needed. Silas replies, "It's a woman, she's dead I think—dead in the snow at the Stone Pits—not far from my door." Nancy Lammeter asks Godfrey who the child is. Godfrey says he does not know.

> **COMMENT:** In the sudden excitement, Godfrey is not sure that the child is his.

Mrs. Kimble tells Silas to leave the child at the Red House but Silas refuses; saying that the child came to him and he has a right to keep her.

> **COMMENT:** Here is the first attempt by Silas to assert his right to the child. It indicates that his long dormant love for people may be ignited again by the child. Later, we shall find that further attempts will be made to separate them.

Dr. Kimble puts on his boots and sends word to have Dolly Winthrop meet him at the Stone Pits. Godfrey, determined to find out if the woman is his wife, tells the doctor he will fetch Dolly. Later, at the cottage of Silas Marner, Godfrey waits outside while Dr. Kimble and Dolly try to save Molly. Godfrey walks up and down in the snow thinking:

(1) He is afraid, if it is his wife, that everything will now be revealed to his father and Nancy,

(2) His next thought is that he should announce to everyone that he is the father of the child and to claim her from Silas Marner. However, he lacks the moral courage to perform such actions.

(3) Finally, he judges that, if this woman were his wife and if she dies, he will finally be free to marry Nancy!

At last, Dr. Kimble comes out to announce that the woman is dead. He mentions, also, that she is wearing a wedding ring on her finger. Kimble leaves and Godfrey enters to see the dead face on the pillow. It is Molly Farren, his wife; the look on her face will haunt Godfrey for years to come. Near the fire, sits Silas Marner . . . lulling the child. Godfrey asks Silas if he plans to surrender the child to the parish authorities in the village. Marner refuses; arguing that no one has a right to take the child away. "I reckon it's got no father," he tells Godfrey.

> **COMMENT:** Notice the irony of the remark that Silas makes to Godfrey about the child not having a father.

Godfrey gives Silas some money for the child and returns to the party at the Red House. He thinks that, perhaps now, he will be able to marry Nancy for:

(1) His wife is dead.
(2) The record of his marriage will probably be forgotten; buried in the pages of a book in a distant village.
(3) He can always bribe Dunstan to remain silent if he returns.
(4) His child will be provided for; he will not forsake it.

PART ONE, CHAPTER FOURTEEN

The burial of Molly Farren that week, in a pauper's grave, attracts no attention in Raveloe or in Batherly where she and her child had lived. Silas Marner's resolve to keep the child leads people to become more sympathetic towards him, although many mothers wonder how he will manage. Dolly Winthrop brings baby clothes which had been Aaron's and gives the child a bath. Dolly offers to care for the child each morning but Silas declines saying, "I want to do things for it myself, else it may get fond o'somebody else, and not fond o'me." Understanding how much Silas loves the child, Dolly tells Silas to put the clothes on the child "and then you can say you've done for her from the first of her coming to you."

> **COMMENT:** Once more, Silas asserts his independence with the child although he is not unwilling to share her with others to an extent.

Dolly cautions Silas about minding the child. Silas says he will tie her to the loom with a long strip of "something" during the day when he is weaving. Mrs. Winthrop promises to bring some pieces of red cloth and other objects for her to play with. Then, she urges Silas to have the child christened. Silas does not know that christening is baptism; a religious ceremony in which the child receives a name and entrance into the church. When he finally understands, his fear of christening leaves him and he consents to have the child called Hephzibah after his younger sister (who died as a child). Dolly does not object to the name because Silas tells her it appears in the Bible but she wonders if it is not a "hard" name. Silas tells her that he called his sister "Eppie."

The child is indeed christened by the Rector. He knows that there is a chance that the child has already been christened but he judges it to be a greater risk not to baptized than to risk baptizing her twice. Silas begins to attend church again because Dolly says it is for the good of the child. Months pass and, unlike Silas' dead gold which was hidden away, Eppie loves sunshine and living things. The gold has led Silas' thoughts, in a circle, back to more thoughts of gold; Eppie now makes his thoughts move forward to the future. The gold has made Silas sit all day at his loom; Eppie calls him away to carry her to the meadows where the flowers grow. She plucks the flowers and, listens to the notes of a bird's song. Silas begins to look for herbs again as he used to do years before.

> **COMMENT:** The change that Eppie brings into the life of Silas is perhaps the most important theme in the novel. George Eliot was very much impressed by the lines which William Wordsworth, the Romantic poet, had written. "A child more than any of the gifts offered to declining man / Brings with it hope and forward-looking thoughts." It is apparent how the author has constructed the novel, up to this point, to show us a man (Silas Marner) who has dried up all the love in his heart. Now, however, through the effect that Eppie has upon him, his spirit will again awaken. George Eliot thought that warm, human relationships between people had a remedial effect; that is, a person whose spirit might be ill because of loss, disappointment or despair could, through the bonds of human love and affection, find hope for the future.

Dolly Winthrop, fearing that Silas is too indulgent with Eppie, suggests that she be punished when she misbehaves. She had four boys of her own and did not hesitate to make certain areas of their anatomy tingle occasionally. But Silas does not wish to hurt Eppie. Dolly tells him of how she used to lock Aaron in the coal bin for a few minutes as a disciplinary measure. One day, Silas tries to use the coal bin for Eppie. As he planned, Silas ties Eppie to his loom each morning with a strip of linen cloth. One morning, Eppie, reaching up and taking a pair of scissors, cuts herself free. Not until Silas needs his scissors does he notice that Eppie is gone! He runs from the house shouting her name. He fears she may have fallen into the stone pits. Perhaps, she has crawled through the fence and is over in the Osgoods' fields. Silas searches one meadow, crosses another fence into a second and, finally, when his hope is almost gone, he discovers Eppie by the edge of a small pond; happily playing in the mud. Silas embraces her; sobbing in relief and happiness. Upon his return to the cottage, however, he decides to punish her by putting her into the coal-hole (a small closet for fuel near the hearth). Eppie enters happily . . . much to his surprise. Silas holds the door closed. All is silent until Eppie cries out, "Opy, Opy." Silas lets her out hoping that the punishment has worked. Eppie is black from the dirt in the coal hole, so Silas spends time washing and dressing her. Silas decides he will not need a new linen band with which tie her. He turns his back for a moment. Suddenly he sees Eppie, her hands and face black once more, peeping out of the coal-hole. She says, "Eppie in the coal-hole!"

> **COMMENT:** In this warm, humorous scene, we find that Silas is an specially warm and kind person. We also judge that Eppie will grow up without very much punishment.

Silas takes Eppie with him whenever he goes out; they become known and liked by everyone in Raveloe. Everyone wants them to sit and talk. Much advice is given to Silas. Even children are not afraid of approaching Silas now that Eppie is with him. Silas enjoys the company, realizing that he must find out, from others, as much as he can so that he may become a better father to Eppie. She is like a plant and he must know all he can about the weather and soil so that she will grow up strong and free from harm. Silas never misses his money now; nor could he ever feels strongly about it as he did formerly, for now he has Eppie. She gives real purpose to his earnings now; hope and joy carrying him beyond any monetary thoughts.

SUMMARY: Opening on a sombre note with the funeral of Molly Farren, the chapter shows, primarily, the great transformation in Silas caused by the child Eppie. Moreover, we notice:

(1) Silas has the child christened and begins to go to church again.
(2) Eppie is mischievious at times but Silas is simply unable to be severe with her. His attempt to discipline her by placing her in the coal-hole backfires. Finally he accepts the truth that she will be reared without any punishment.

At the close of the chapter, George Eliot uses a metaphor taken from the Bible to express part of her purpose in writing the novel. In earlier times, there were angels who came and took men by the hand and led them away from the city of destruction. Although there are no white-winged angels now, men can be led away from threatening destruction: a hand is put in theirs and leads them to a calm and bright land; the hand may be a child's. Once again, the author repeats the idea that a small child has the power to give man a sense of promise and expectation. Eppie is Silas' hope for the future.

PART ONE, CHAPTER FIFTEEN

Godfrey Cass watches, with hidden interest, the growth of his child, Eppie, under the care of the weaver. Occasionally, he gives a present to Silas but he knows he must be careful not to arouse suspicion. He does not wish people to wonder why he is interested in the welfare of a poor man and his adopted child. Godfrey does not feel uneasy about leaving his child to be reared by another. He excuses his attitude by telling himself that children brought up in humble surroundings are often happier than those brought up in luxury.

Godfrey does feel regret (but it is seldom) for now his whole attitude toward life has changed. He seems happier. Dunstan has not returned; perhaps he has joined the army and left the country. No one cares nor asks about him. Godfrey stops worrying about him. Almost every day of the week, he can be seen riding to the Warrens' house to see Nancy.

> **COMMENT:** Remember that Godfrey is free to marry Nancy because his wife, Molly Farren, is dead.

Godfrey has visions of marrying Nancy and can picture himself playing with his children at the hearth. As far as Eppie is concerned, he will see that she is always provided for; but he will never reveal that she is his daughter.

PART TWO, CHAPTER ONE

Sixteen years have passed. Eppie is about eighteen years old and Silas is about fifty-five. It is a bright autumn Sunday in Raveloe and we see the villagers coming out of the old church across the street from the Red House. Godfrey Cass, one of the most important men in Raveloe, is among the first to leave. With him, is his pretty wife, Nancy. They have been married for fifteen years but have no children. The Squire has died and his inheritance has been divided among his sons; all except Dunstan, who has disappeared long ago. Walking behind Godfrey and Nancy are Priscilla Lammeter and her father, who is now quite aged. Priscilla never married, preferring to remain independent. They still live at their estate, the Warrens, but they are going to the Red House to have Sunday dinner with Godfrey and Nancy. Among the others in the congregation are Silas Marner and Eppie. Silas, with his white hair and stooped shoulders looks like a much older man than he actually is. Eppie is a very dainty and beautiful girl with a light complexion, curly reddish-brown hair and dimples. Walking behind Eppie is Aaron Winthrop, now a good-looking young gardener of twenty-three.

He is listening to the conversation between Eppie and Silas. Eppie tells her old father that she wishes that they had a little garden like Dolly Winthrop (Aaron's mother) has at her cottage.

COMMENT: The second part of the novel occurs after an extended period of time. Look for the changes in people as George Eliot describes them. We find that Godfrey Cass has married Nancy but that they have no children. The Squire is dead; Dunsey has never returned; Priscilla and her father live at the Warrens but often visit Nancy and Godfrey at the Red House. Eppie has not been claimed by Godfrey as his daughter so Silas has been her father. He has told her that he found her mother dead in the snow and that no ones knows who her real father is. Now, she is very lovely. Her suggestion that she would like a garden such as Dolly Winthrop has may be a hint that she would like to have the company of Aaron Winthrop. He would probably dig it for her.

Silas agrees to have a garden; he can dig it in the morning and in the evening when he is not working at his loom. He wonders why Eppie has not mentioned this to him before. Suddenly, Aaron comes forward and exclaims that he can dig the garden instead of Silas. He will be able to find time during the slack in work at the Red House where he is Godfrey Cass' gardener; or else after work. He tells Silas that he will ask to bring soil from Godfrey's garden, also. Eppie tells Silas that he should do only the light work in the garden with her; she plans to have rosemary, bergamot and thyme. Aaron tells her he will bring lavender from Godfrey's garden. She says she thinks: "The flowers can see us and know what we're talking about." Silas does not want to ask for anything more from Mr. Cass because Godfrey has already been very generous to him and Eppie; building a new addition to their cottage. Aaron explains that the flowers can easily be spared and he observes that, if all good farming land was used, for example, no one need go hungry in the world. Eppie asks Aaron to bring Dolly to the stone pits, also, because she can advise them about the garden. Aaron leaves. Eppie happily skips for she knows that Aaron likes her and that he will dig the garden for her. Silas and Eppie are greeted by one of their donkeys as they approach their cottage at the stone pits.

Inside, they are met by their brown terrier, Snap. A cat and a kitten are their other pets. The beautiful oak furniture in their cottage is the gift of Godfrey Cass. Eppie prepares their Sunday meal and Silas watches as she feeds the animals. Later, he goes outside to smoke. Silas has begun smoking for the past two years on the advice of the so-called wise men of the village. (Mr. Macey is still giving advice at eighty-six. He predicts that Silas will some day have his money returned.)

COMMENT: Silas and Eppie live a quiet and simple life. Together, they have happily passed the years with their friends and their pets. The author now employs a summary of what has occurred during the past sixteen years as far as certain attitudes of Silas are concerned.

Silas smokes a pipe because other people in Raveloe advise him to do so. Through force of habit, Silas has become used to following the advice of his neighbors because, when he first found Eppie on his hearth years before, he knew the only way he could manage was to listen to what others told him about what to do for her. He began to trust in his neighbors; wondering if, perhaps, there might have been some error in his thinking, as a young man, when he lost his faith in God and Man after the drawing of the lots which had found him guilty of the robbery at Lantern Yard. Over the years, he had gradually revealed to Dolly Winthrop the circumstances of his early life. Dolly did not understand quickly, needing repeated explanations of what happened before she comprehended the absurd plan of drawing the lots to find if Silas were guilty or innocent. She thought, perhaps, that Silas belonged to a totally different kind of religion but Silas assured her that he used the same Bible at Lantern Yard that Dolly used. Dolly was confused and, although admitting that she did not have the power to understand it as well as "wise folks" like the parson might, she told Silas that if "Them above" (God) had been fair to Silas, he would have been found innocent. Silas explained to Dolly that, because he was found guilty and his friend William Dane had "framed" him, he lost his faith. Dolly said Dane was truly a "bad 'un" and brought up the subject of the lots again. This time, she said that those who drew the lots (except for William Dane) probably thought they had done the right thing but God knew the truth of Silas' innocence, regardless of their verdict. Dolly admitted that suffering and pain come into the world and many things occur which can never be satisfactorily explained but she concluded: "all as we've got to do is trusten, Master Marner—to do the right thing as fur as we know, and to trusten." If Silas could have gone on trusting in God after he had been so disappointed, he might never have run away from his fellow human beings and become so lonely. Silas agreed that trusting would have been difficult but that it would have been "right." He recognized now that there was good in the world along with the evil. The drawing of the lots was "dark," but Eppie was sent to him, so there is a certain kind of justice: "there's dealings with us—there's dealings."

COMMENT: By talking to Dolly Winthrop about his past, Silas has been able to see the reasons why he gave up hope and why it was a mistake to judge God and all human beings so harshly because of the plotting of William Dane and the misguided judgment of his Lantern Yard brethren.

Silas had also often talked to Eppie about the past. This was when she became mature enough to understand. He did not wish her to find out about her past through the gossip of Raveloe neighbors. Eppie was told about how her mother had died on the snowy ground and how she herself had been found on the hearth by Silas—who had mistaken her golden curls for his gold.

Eppie had not even thought about her real father until the day Silas gave her the wedding ring which had been taken from the wasted finger of Molly Farren. She kept it in a small shoe-shaped box and, when she looked at it, she did not think of her father but of her mother. She often asked Silas how she looked and whom she was like.

> **COMMENT:** Silas has wisely told Eppie about her past. She feels no love for any father but often asks Silas about her dead mother. Both she and Silas do not realize, of course, that Godfrey is her true father.

On that same Sunday (sixteen years later) Eppie joins Silas. He is now outside of the cottage smoking his pipe. Eppie asks Silas if they can transplant (to the new garden) the furze bush on which Molly Farren, her mother, had lain the night she died. Silas agrees; also suggesting that a fence must be erected to prevent their donkeys and the other animals from trampling everything in the garden. Since a fence, however, is an expensive item, Eppie suggests that a wall of stones be built instead. Silas and Aaron can gather the larger stones and she the smaller ones. To demonstrate her rock-carrying ability, Eppie skips over to the stone pits, then calls to Silas, "O father, come and see ho wthe water's gone down since yesterday. Why, yesterday, the pit was ever so full!" Silas explains that the pit is being drained so that the water may be transferred to Mr. Osgood's field, which is next to Silas' cottage and has now been taken over by Godfrey Cass.

> **COMMENT:** The draining of the stone pits is a significant incident for it will change the lives of Godfrey, Nancy, Silas, and Eppie.

Eppie, sitting on a bank with Silas in the shadows of the late afternoon, suggests gently that she has been thinking of marrying. She introduces this thought by asking Silas if she should wear her mother's wedding ring if she ever marries. Silas has thought that someday she might marry and he now asks her if Aaron wants to marry her. Hoping Silas will consent, Eppie admits it; telling Silas that she is in love with him and that he is prospering as a gardener with work at the Red House, Mr. Osgood's, and soon, at the Rectory. Eppie explains that both Aaron and she would expect Silas to live with them after they are married. Eppie has told Aaron that she is happy with her present life and Aaron has made her cry by telling her that if she really loves him she would marry him.

COMMENT: Eppie is faced with a problem of divided love:

(1) She loves Silas; yet, she wishes to marry Aaron.

(2) Eppie's love for Aaron is strong but her love for Silas makes her want to stay with him; even though Aaron has shown his love for the weaver by wanting him to live with them after they are married. Eppie is hoping, primarily, that Silas will accept Aaron as her husband and consent to live with them.

Silas lays down his pipe; saying that Eppie is "young to get married." He suggests that Mrs. Winthrop be asked for her opinion. Yet, Silas recognizes that things do change in life; someday, he will be older and more helpless. He has thought that it would be a comforting thing to know that someone young and strong would then be able to care for Eppie. **"Then, would you like me to be married, father?" Eppie asks, with** a little trembling in her voice. Silas tells her he will consent to her marriage but that Dolly Winthrop, Eppie's godmother at her baptism, must also consent. Just then, Eppie sees Dolly and Aaron coming to the cottage.

SUMMARY: In this long first chapter of the second part of the novel we discover that sixteen years have elapsed since the night that Silas first discovered Eppie. Several important developments have occurred in this long passage of time:

(1) Godfrey has married Nancy. His first marriage is still a secret. No one ever discovered that he had been married to Molly Farren, the unidentified woman found in the snow.

(2) Silas has become the only father Eppie has ever known although her true father, Godfrey, has helped her and Silas financially through the years.

(3) Dunsey Cass has never returned. His whereabouts are unknown. Later in the chapter, we find that Eppie wishes to build a garden and that Aaron Winthrop (who once came to visit Silas with his mother shortly after the robbery) is the man she loves. Eppie reveals her love for Aaron to her father. We also perceive, in this chapter, an attempt by Dolly Winthrop to explain the reasons for Marner's loss of faith to him. She tells him, essentially, that his mistake is to blame God and all men for the willful plotting of William Dane and the poor judgment of the others in choosing lots to find Silas guilty. Silas realizes, as Dolly points out, that the important thing to do in times of great disappointment and loss, is "to trusten"; to have faith in God. One new incident, which will become significant, is the draining of water from the stone pits.

PART TWO, CHAPTER TWO

Meanwhile, at the Red House on the same Sunday afternoon, Priscilla Lammeter and her father are preparing to leave for their home after having dinner with Nancy and Godfrey. The parlour of the Red House has changed since the days when Squire Cass was alive.

(1) Everything is now polished and is dusted every day.

(2) All sporting equipment, guns, whips, etc., have been carefully hung on the antlers of a stuffed stag over the fireplace. The tankards gleam untouched because they are always empty.

(3) The smell of stale ale has been replaced by lavender and rose-leaves.

All has been purity and order in the Red House since Godfrey married Nancy, fifteen years ago. Nancy asks her father to stay but he permits Priscilla to answer for him since she "manages" him and his business on the farm. This because of his advanced age. Priscilla wishes to leave, without staying for tea, because she must return to the Warrens to be certain that one of their dairymaids (who is soon to be married) performs her tasks properly. As the horses are being readied, Priscilla tells Nancy that she is glad that Godfrey had decided to enter the dairy business; for it will keep her occupied and free from melancholy thoughts.

> **COMMENT:** Priscilla knows that Nancy and Godfrey are disappointed because they have had no children.

Priscilla knows that Godfrey also has been restless because they are childless and suggests to Nancy that she could have remained single. Nancy defends Godfrey by saying it is natural that Godfrey should be disappointed; otherwise, "He's the best of husbands." The gig (carriage) approaches. It is drawn by the Lammeters' horse, Speckle, and Priscilla leaves with her father. Nancy begins to read her Bible while Godfrey goes for his accustomed Sunday afternoon walk. Alone with her thoughts about her life with Godfrey, Nancy feels that Godfrey suffers because they have had no children much more than she does. Nancy had lost a baby early in their marriage and, although she still has a drawer full of baby clothes, all unworn, she refuses to permit herself to complain about the baby's death. She never opens the drawer for she feels she would be wishing for something that was not meant to happen. She wonders now if she has done the right thing for Godfrey by refusing, six years ago, to adopt Eppie.

> **COMMENT:** There are four reasons why Nancy did not wish to adopt a child:

(1) People in the early nineteenth century were less ready to rear

children who were not their own than people are today. Adopti was a much rarer practice then than it is now.

(2) Nancy felt that it would be against the will of Providence to hav children if they were not their own.

(3) Because of her rigid code and inflexible nature, once Nancy had determined upon a course of action, she would not change. We recall how strictly she adhered to her habits: years earlier, at the dance at the Red House, she insisted upon wearing the same kind of dress as Priscilla because "it was right for sisters to dress alike." Nancy is meticulous in her dress and personal belongings. Every article in her home is in its proper place. Her lack of deviation from a fixed or ordered pattern causes her to become rigid in her opinions. She thinks it wrong to adopt a child because God did not give her one; she will continue to think that way.

(4) Nancy is somewhat superstitious. For example, she would not make a purchase at a particular place if, on three successive occasions, rain or some obstacle had prevented her from going. She views such happenings as warnings from heaven.

This last reason of Nancy's is commented upon by George Eliot (who was not a member of a formal religion) as an instance of how human belief can arrive at a truth akin to a belief which is theological. In other words, the author is saying that ideas of a human can equal the ideas of a religion. One belief comes from man; the other from God. We may infer that the author does not believe in the supernatural dogma of Christianity.

Years earlier, when Eppie was about twelve, Godfrey had told Nancy that he wanted to adopt her (never realizing how Silas and Eppie felt about each other!) Nancy had refused, hoping that he would understand. Godfrey admired Nancy for the strength of her conviction concerning Eppie and, although he was disappointed, he accepted it. Naturally, he knew that he could never tell Nancy that Eppie was his own child and he felt that their childless state now was more or less a retribution for his abandonment of her to Silas when she was a child.

Nancy, sitting alone, wonders how lonely Godfrey would be if she died. Suddenly, a servant (Jane) informs her mistress that she has seen a number of people "making haste" down the road; she ends by saying, "I hope nobody's been hurt that's all." Nancy, wishing that Jane would not terrify her so, thinks that perhaps a bull has broken loose. She walks to the window and gazes out; hoping for Godfrey's return, yet, sensing a strange fear.

SUMMARY: We find that Nancy and Godfrey cannot find complete marital happiness because they have no children. Nancy is resigned to this truth because she accepts it as God's will but Godfrey is restless. Their first child died and, later, Nancy refused to adopt Eppie because of her rigid opinions. Godfrey began to see his childless marriage as retribution for his permitting Silas to rear Eppie; his own child.

PART TWO, CHAPTER THREE

Just then, the door opens and Godfrey enters. He is pale and motions Nancy to be seated. Jane leaves the room and the trembling Godfrey begins to speak: "I've had a great shock." Nancy becomes frightened; fearing that something has happened to her father and Priscilla. Godfrey answers, "It's Dunstan — my brother . . . we've found him — found his body — his skeleton." Nancy feels somewhat relieved open hearing that the news was not about her father and Priscilla. Godfrey explains that the stone pit has suddenly gone dry. This was probably from draining it for the land Godfrey had bought from Mr. Osgood for his future dairy farm. Dunstan's body has lain for sixteen years, wedged tightly between two great stones. This prevented him from saving himself. His watch and Godfrey's gold-handled riding whip, which Dunstan had borrowed the day he went to sell Wildfire, are found. The name Godfrey Cass is inscribed on the handle of the whip. Godfrey pauses. Nancy asks if Dunstan had drowned himself. "No, he fell in," Godfrey answers, adding, "Dunstan was the man that robbed Silas Marner." Nancy blushes, ashamed at the dishonor she feels. She sympathizes for Godfrey who continues by explaining that the money which Dunstan had stolen from the cottage of Silas Marner also has been found.

> **COMMENT:** We learn that several significant facts are discovered by Godfrey and Nancy in this chapter:
> (1) Dunsey is dead.
> (2) He is the thief who stole Marner's money.
> (3) Silas' money has been found. His fortune will be returned to him.

Nancy senses that Godfrey has something else to tell her: Godfrey admits that he has been living with a secret on his mind for years but, now, he will tell her. Nancy is frightened again. Godfrey reveals that the woman Silas found dead in the snow, "Eppie's mother—that wretched woman—was my wife: Eppie is my child." Nancy is silent. Godfrey tries to defend himself. He explains that he knew he should not have left the child unowned yet he was afraid to tell Nancy earlier because he might lose her. Nancy looks at Godfrey and answers regretfully that, if he had only told her that Eppie was his child six years ago, they could have done their duty by her. "Do you think I'd have refused to take her in knowing she was yours?" Nancy asks. She tells Godfrey she would have taken Eppie in as a baby and cared for her as her own child. It would have been easier for her to bear the loss of her own baby and both she and Godfrey would have been happier in their marriage.

> **COMMENT:** It is ironic that, when Godfrey finally reveals the secret marriage which he hesitated to do for years (because he feared losing Nancy), he finds, contrary to his expectation, that she would have welcomed the child. Here is an example of Godfrey's inability to understand the true worth of his wife. His error in judgment has resulted in two bitter consequences:
> (1) The secret about Eppie was discovered eventually although he concealed it.
> (2) Because he concealed it, Nancy did not know that Eppie was his child and refused to adopt her. Thus, both of them lost years of happiness with her.

Nancy begins to cry. Godfrey attempts to defend his action explaining to Nancy that he was afraid to tell her years earlier because of her pride and her father's great pride; she would have hated him. Nancy admits to Godfrey that she doesn't know what she would have done but she wouldn't have married anyone else. She adds: "But I wasn't worth doing wrong for—nothing is in this world." Nancy smiles sadly admitting that even their marriage was not as good as Godfrey had expected it would be. Nancy feels that the person most injured is Eppie; both agree to adopt her into their home. Plans are made to visit Silas Marner's house as soon as everything is quiet down at the stone pits.

SUMMARY: In this brief, but revelatory chapter, much light is shed on past events and much speculation is created about the future. The disappearance of Dunsey Cass is finally explained; Marner is a rich man again; Godfrey has at last revealed his two-fold secret:
(1) His marriage to Molly Farren, the woman found dead at the Stone Pits.
(2) Eppie is his child.

Nancy is shocked and disappointed; she tells Godfrey that she would have agreed to adopt Eppie if she had only known that she was Godfrey's child. She senses that their marriage has not been as happy as it could have been. We wonder what the reaction of Marner and Eppie will be, now that Nancy and Godfrey have decided to adopt Eppie.

PART TWO, CHAPTER FOUR

In Silas Marner's cottage that night, he and Eppie are discussing the events of the day. Aaron and his mother, Mrs. Winthrop, are the last people to leave after the excitement of discovering Dunsey Cass' body and Silas' gold. Numerous people were into the cottage; now, Silas and

Eppie are alone. The gold is arranged in orderly heaps on a table. Silas has been sitting in the candlelight, telling Eppie of how he used to count it every night and how desolate he was until she was "sent" to him; he explains how much she came to mean to him. Eppie says, "If it hadn't been for you, they'd have taken me to the workhouse and there's been nobody to love me." Silas sits in silence for a few minutes looking at the money and wondering if it ever could "take a hold" of him again. Silas is afraid that, if he lost Eppie, he might think that he was forsaken again and lose the feeling that God was good to him.

> **COMMENT:** The discovery of the gold causes Silas to consider his values. Never can the money replace the happiness Silas has found with Eppie. Yet, he fears that, if he should ever lose Eppie, he might return to his eccentric habits of counting it each night.

Just then, there is a knocking at the door. Eppie opens the door for Mr. and Mrs. Godfrey Cass and curtsies to them as they enter. Nancy apologizes for coming so late. (It is between eight and nine o'clock.) She and Godfrey sit opposite Silas and Eppie. Uneasily, Godfrey begins to explain why he and his wife have come to visit. He tells Silas that it is a comfort to him to see the money returned; especially since someone in his family had stolen it. He almost blurts out that he is also indebted to Silas for caring for his child, Eppie, but he and Nancy had agreed that the secret of her real fatherhood should not be disclosed to Eppie, if possible, until the future. Godfrey suggests to Silas that he is growing older (Silas admits he is fifty-five) and since, after all, the money was returned to him but couldn't last forever, perhaps he would like to see Eppie well provided for. Godfrey is clearly expressing a wish to take Eppie into his family and to have her live at the Red House. Silas, however, is unsure of Godfrey's intention. "I don't take your meaning, sir," he answers.

Godfrey explains that he and his wife would like to have Eppie as their daughter. While he is speaking, Eppie slips her hand behind her father's head; Silas is trembling. When Godfrey finishes, Silas speaks to Eppie, telling her that he "won't stand in her way" if she wishes to go to live with Mr. and Mrs. Cass.

Eppie gives a low curtesy and thanks Godfrey and Nancy telling them, "I can't leave my father." She adds, "I don't want to be a lady—thank you all the same." She retreats to her father's chair and puts her hand around his neck.

Godfrey finally admits, in desperation, that he is Eppie's father. "She's my own child: her mother was my wife." Godfrey feels that his natural claim on his daughter supercedes all others.

> **COMMENT:** Notice how Godfrey fails to appreciate other people's feelings. He does not realize how much suffering Silas would experience if Eppie were to leave him.

Silas demands bitterly to know why Godfrey did not admit his fatherhood sixteen years earlier before he (Silas) had come to love her. He tells Godfrey that God gave Eppie to him because Godfrey had turned his back on her. He then concludes by observing: "When a man turns a blessing from his door, it falls to them as take it in."

> **COMMENT:** Here is another theme which echoes the adage about opportunity knocking but once.

Godfrey admits that he was wrong but defends his position by saying he has repented of his earlier refusal to accept and acknowledge Eppie. Silas refuses to accept mere repentance because it doesn't "alter the feelings inside us." Godfrey is awed at the truth of Silas' words but continues his plea for Eppie. Silas refuses again. Godfrey is becoming angry slowly. He begins to assert his authority; accusing Silas of standing in the way of Eppie's welfare. He concludes that it is his "duty" to insist on taking care of his own daughter.

Eppie is thinking of her past life with Silas and what a future life with Godfrey as her father would be like. She is repelled by the thought of accepting Godfrey's offer. Silas, on the other hand, is unsure in his conscience. Is he actually retarding the way of Eppie's happiness? Finally he speaks, saying that he will leave the decision to Eppie, "I'll hinder nothing."

Nancy breathes a sigh of relief, assuming that any poor person like Eppie would naturally be anxious to receive the benefits of a wealthier life. She feels as Godfrey does; that their wish is achieved. Both of them tell Eppie how much she will mean to them. "You'll be a treasure to me," Nancy tells her.

Once more, Eppie steps forward to curtsy. After thanking them again, Eppie then speaks with a colder decision than previously. She utterly refuses to leave her father; explaining that, without him, she could never be happy. Silas has loved her from the first and nobody shall ever come between them. Silas asks Eppie to be sure; she replies that she can never be sorry because she never cared for the "fine things" such as clothes, a carriage, or a place in church (a special, reserved pew).

Nancy, seeing that Godfrey has no reply, cautions Eppie that she should accept the offer of her lawful father; but Eppie, her eyes welling with tears, disagrees about the idea and tells her that the only "father" she believes she ever had is Silas. In the midst of tears, Eppie reveals her strong love for "a workingman" and her engagement to him.

Godfrey's face is flushed and he is unable to say anything but "Let us go!" Nancy suggests that they will come and visit again.

SUMMARY: The attempts of Godfrey and Nancy to win Eppie are fruitless. They present several reasons to Silas why Eppie should come:

(1) Godfrey and Nancy have no children and would like to rear Eppie. This reason, however, is rejected. Godfrey therefore argues:

(2) He is the real father of Eppie and has a claim over her. Silas refuses to accept the validity of such a claim because Godfrey has neglected the child for sixteen years. Godfrey appeals to Silas and Eppie on the grounds that:

(3) He can give Eppie advantages which only a wealthy girl can have. Silas is ready to admit this truth leaving the decision to Eppie; She decisively rejects the offer because:

(4) She is unaccustomed to luxuries.

(5) She is engaged to be married to a workingman. (She does not specify Aaron by name.)

PART TWO, CHAPTER FIVE

Nancy and Godfrey walk home in the starlight. When they enter the Red House, Godfrey sits in a chair and says "That's ended." Nancy agrees; it would be wrong for them to force Eppie to come against her will. Godfrey sadly remembers what Silas said about a man's turning a blessing from his door: it falls to somebody else. Nancy asks Godfrey if he will make it known that Eppie is his daughter but Godfrey refuses; judging that no possible good can come from such a revelation. He is more concerned with helping her after her marriage; he guesses correctly that she is probably in love with Aaron for he remembers seeing them come out of church together.

Nancy is relieved that her sister Priscilla and her father will never learn of Eppie's real father. She also observes that Aaron is a sober and industrious person. Godfrey determines to leave all the information in his will. He feels sorrow that his daughter disliked him; yet, he accepts it as part of his punishment for his shirking of his duty to her. Nancy tacitly agrees. Her spirit of righteousness does not permit her to soften the edge of what she feels is proper remorse. Nancy asks Godfrey to become resigned to this which is their lot in life. Godfrey agrees it may not be too late to learn to accept the way things are but he does regret that it is too late to mend "some" things.

COMMENT: The theme of this chapter is acceptance. Godfrey and Nancy, after returning home and considering the refusal of

Eppie to become their charge, learn to accept her decision. Godfrey will keep his parenthood a secret until he dies. Both he and Nancy can accept Aaron as her husband. Together, they will live out their lives without children; hoping to help Eppie when they can but realizing that it is too late to change the truth of Godfrey's earlier treatment of her.

PART TWO, CHAPTER SIX

The next morning, at breakfast, Silas suggests to Eppie that they set out the following day on a journey to Lantern Yard where Silas had been accused of the theft of the dead Deacon's money. Silas wishes:
(1) to discover if any proof of his innocence has been discovered.
(2) to speak to a Mr. Paston (who was the minister) about the drawing of the lots.
(3) to discuss the religion of the people who live in the country-side; people like those in Raveloe.

Eppie is happy to go so that she can recount the trip to Aaron; since he seems to know so much about things. She considers it a small "advantage" that she will be able to tell him something. Mrs. Winthrop, assured that the journey will not be a perilous one, is well pleased that Silas should visit his native place to find out if he has been finally cleared of the mistaken guilt for the robbery.

Four days later, Silas and Eppie are walking in the streets of a large manufacturing town; looking for that section of the town called Lantern Yard. Eppie, seeing a gentleman standing in a doorway, asks Silas to inquire from him the directions to Lantern Yard but Silas refuses stating that the gentlemen of the town would not know of its existence. Silas does receive directions to the jail, however, and he and Eppie proceed to turn left three blocks past it. After a few more turns, they come to Shoe Lane and proceed to a street near an overhanging window.

All the while they have been walking, Eppie and her father have been shocked by the dreary aspect of the town. Eppie calls it a "dark, ugly" place. She is "stifled" by the way the people live so closely together and thinks of how delightful it will be to return to the Stone Pits. Even Silas notices a change. The air smells bad but it "usened" (used) to smell differently years before. Occasionally, a grimy face peers at them from a doorway; such glances only increase Eppie's uneasiness.

Suddenly, Silas stops short; there is an amazed look on his face. They are standing before the exit of a large factory through which men and women are hurrying on their way to lunch. Finally, Silas says, "It's gone, child. Lantern Yard's gone." Indeed, a large factory has replaced the area in which the chapel, the graveyard, and the buildings where Lantern Yard stood had been. Eppie, afraid that Silas may suffer one of his cataleptic attacks, leads him to a little brush shop so that he may sit down. However, no one can tell Marner anything more than that the factory was ten years old; nothing is known of any of his old friends or of Mr. Paston the minister.

When Silas and Eppie return to Raveloe, Silas tells Dolly Winthrop that, now, he will never know whether Mr. Paston could have given him any information about the drawing of the lots. Marner is resigned to the probability that it will remain "dark to the last"; that is, until he dies. Dolly agrees observing that "them above" (God) have many things they prefer should remain "dark" to men. The simple things in living and the daily tasks she faces are the aspects of life which Dolly understands: "mostly what comes i' the day's work." She concludes that Silas was unjustly treated once and, to be sure, he will never know the reason for it; yet, that does not hinder there being a reason for it even if "it's all dark" or incapable of being understood. Silas agrees with Dolly saying that, since Eppie has come to him, he has had enough light to "trusten by" (hope in God) and, now that Eppie has told him that he will live with her and Aaron after they are married, Silas believes he will "trusten" until he dies.

SUMMARY: Over thirty years have elapsed since Silas left Lantern Yard. George Eliot pictures his return in a manner which echoes Washington Irving's *Rip Van Winkle.* Both men return to their former villages (decades after leaving them) to be greeted with numerous changes. England, at the time of Silas and Eppie, was undergoing the beginning of a vast number of technological and social changes caused by the first rumblings of the industrial revolution of the nineteenth century. Compare this chapter with the first to see how the author expresses the differences in life for men at the beginning of the century, "when spinning wheels hummed busily" with the great changes wrought by machines a mere thirty years later. The city is beginning to replace the country as a home for most men; the skilled worker, with his craft and pride in creating excellence in his products, is disappearing; his son is probably working long hours in a large brick factory performing a routine, unchallenging job in a mass-producing business.

Silas is lost in such a world and he returns gratefully to Raveloe. Although he has not been successful in determining anything new about his past experience at Lantern Yard, he reveals (in his discussion with Dolly Winthrop) an acceptance of life's mysteries; we notice that this acceptance theme had a parallel in the previous chapter as Godfrey and Nancy agreed to face their future without hope of having Eppie.

CONCLUSION

Springtime in Raveloe was always considered an especially appropriate time for a wedding. The ornamental flowers, such as the yellow laburnum shrubs and the April lilacs, are blowing. Eppie is seen going by the Red House and into the church with one arm on Aaron; the other is on her father. She is wearing a light, white cotton dress with a pink sprig at the side; the gown is a gift from Mrs. Cass. Her hair looks as if it is the dash of gold found on a lily. Miss Priscilla Lammeter and her father pull up in their carriage just in time to see the bridal party, which also includes Ben and Dolly Winthrop who enter the church. Priscilla and her father agree it is unfortunate that Nancy never had a child. Just then Nancy comes out and Priscilla and her father meet her. Neither Nancy or Godfrey attend the ceremony. Godfrey is out of town on "business" in Lytherly but he has ordered a wedding feast for the bridal party and the townspeople at the Rainbow Tavern.

As the wedding party passes Mr. Macey (who is sitting outside his own door in an armchair) they stop on the advice of Dolly who knows he is too old to attend the wedding feast. Mr. Macey has a few things to say to Silas; chiefly that he has lived to see his prediction come true that Silas would receive his money again.

In the open yard of the Rainbow Tavern, the guests have assembled although it is still nearly an hour before the wedding reception. The men are discussing Silas Marner's strange story and even Mr. Snell, the farrier (veterinary), agrees that Silas had "brought a blessing upon himself" by adopting and rearing Eppie, an orphaned child. Suddenly, the bridal group is seen approaching the Rainbow and a cheer is given by those assembled there. Ben Winthrop runs out of the bridal party which is coming from the church to the Stone Pits for an hour of quiet before the reception. He shakes hands briefly and exchanges congratulations with the men at the tavern.

Eppie, Aaron, Silas, and Dolly approach the Stone Pits, which will be the new home of Eppie, her husband, and her father. Eppie joyfully exclaims that no one could have been happier than they are!

SUMMARY: The conclusion (although considered by some readers to be unnecessary to the story because it is to be assumed that all will end happily for Silas and Eppie) is nevertheless a pleasant and warm picture of a springtime wedding in rural England.

An interesting insight into how Godfrey and Nancy have decided to act towards Eppie is shown in their refusal to attend the wedding although Nancy has donated the dress and Godfrey has financed the wedding feast. Nancy invites her father and sister to visit so that she cannot attend; it is deliberately arranged for Godfrey to be unavailable at the marriage because of business.

CHARACTER ANALYSES

Silas Marner: Silas Marner, the weaver of Raveloe, represents a kind of craftsman commonly seen in England in the years before the Industrial Revolution. Naturally honest and shy as a young man, Silas finds delight in the friendships he makes in the Lantern Yard church. His sincerity wins the love of Sarah and of his friend William Dane. Because he is a very thorough person, his mental processes appear to be slower than normal, yet, he is able to perceive the plot of Dane against him. His uneducated mind, surrounded by the superstitious aura, does prevent him, however, from interpreting accurately the significance of the drawing of the lots.

Through the loss of faith following his "trial," Silas becomes a cold, distant hermit; submerging those aspects of his nature which companionship had brought to the surface. Perhaps his unrelenting industry is the only one of his traits which endures: through it, and a new trait (avarice), he is able to amass a fortune in savings from weaving. His love of people has been transferred to gold. After the loss of his money, he is compelled to ask his neighbors for assistance; such contacts are multiplied and intensified when he becomes the guardian of Eppie.

Silas indicates strength of character by refusing to part with Eppie when he finds her and when, years later, he is ordered to do so by Godfrey. Although physically a wan, short-sighted man, prone to violent and prolonged cataleptic seizures which make his body rigidly motionless, Silas displays a spiritual inflexibility in his sense of justice and determination to protect Eppie, whose love had unlocked his natural emotions.

Godfrey Cass: Born into wealth, Godfrey Cass loses his mother early in his life and receives no moral guidance from his father, the Squire. Free to idle, he acquires debilitating habits and an irregular, purposeless life. Naturally generous and sincere, he lacks the moral strength to resist the influence of his dissolute younger brother, Dunstan Cass, and is led into a demeaning marriage.

His vacillation is, in part, prompted by fear and, in part, by an unrealistic, inane trust in chance. He remains silent when his wife, Molly Farren, dies and fails to acknowledge Eppie as his child; he justifies his need for future happiness as a reason for denying his child's right to parenthood.

His marriage to Nancy suddenly ends his profigacy; he now leads a correct moral life. His happiness is impaired by the loss of his only child; but it is not until Dunstan's body is discovered that he is prompted to reveal to his wife his relationship to Eppie. When Marner and his daughter refuse what he considers his lawful and magnanimous proposal, to take the child he is chagrined; yet, in time, he accepts the disappointment as a nemesis for his early indifference. That he refrains from attending the wedding feast indicates that he has been considerate enough to avoid Eppie the day of the wedding lest his presence mar her happiness.

William Dane: William Dane is, like Silas, a weaver; he also attends Lantern Yard church and is secretly in love with Silas' fiancee, Sarah. A naturally ambitious and proud man, Dane has predicted his own salvation by reading in a Bible, (he tells his brethren) the words "calling and election sure." His problem is to separate Sarah from Silas. We know that Silas innocently invites him to accompany him on his Sunday walks with Sarah. Dane bides his time until an appropriate situation presents itself. When the minister dies, and he arrives to find Silas in a cataleptic attack, a thought occurs to him: now, he can damage Silas' reputation permanently. He steals the money in the drawer, leaves the knife Silas has given him; to implicate Silas. He then hurries to plant the empty money box in Silas' room. Later, his treacherous advice to Silas is that he "confess." Success comes to him: he later marries Sarah. To win her, he has had only to steal, slander, and destroy the happiness of his friend: Silas Marner.

Nancy Lammeter: The younger daughter of the sober, exemplary widower, Mr. Lammeter, Nancy has a sense of family and propriety characteristic of proper young women in smaller towns. Severe in her own moral code, she could hardly be expected to condone the unstable conduct of a young man unless, of course, he happened to be Mr. Godfrey Cass and she was in love with him. Because Nancy is dignified, reserved, and cautious, Godfrey is hesitant to tell her of his secret marriage. Yet, he knows that she alone can make him happy: she is beautiful, warm, a meticulous housekeeper and will make an exceptional mother. Refined, although she lacks formal cultural attainments, her acceptance of her childless marriage is a result of her childlike superstition and her inflexible religious scruples.

Squire Cass: The Squire is a caricature of a familiar English type: the man of influence in a small village who owes his position more to recognized heredity, wealth and name than to his own accomplishments. He lacks the warmth and humor of the gentle, model types which Addison and Steel had attempted to create as a model in their eighteenth century periodicals. Nor is the Squire the amiable Pickwick type as envisioned by Dickens. Excessive, intemperate and an ill-humored man, his occasional high spirits are merely indicative of his basically irresponsible nature.

Eppie: The true daughter of Godfrey Cass by his first marriage with Molly Farren, Eppie is a beautiful blonde child capable of great affection. She remains loyal to Silas when Godfrey and Nancy wish her to leave him for a wealthier life. A lover of nature, she delights in animals and flowers. Her sheltered, simple life promises to be even happier in her marriage to Aaron Winthrop. Her courage is shown in the crucial scene in which she refuses to recognize Godfrey's rights to her when he and Nancy come to Marner's cottage to claim her.

Priscilla Lammeter: As the older sister of Nancy, she is used as a foil to contrast with Nancy. Naturally plain, she is unconcerned with love or beauty. Utterly candid about herself and her looks, Priscilla believes it is better to be independent than married. Loyal to her father throughout his old age, she is also a shrewd and serious business manager of his estate. Basically a strong and direct person, she understands others only in the most general ways; the humor of her character arises from her complete disregard for the sensitivity of others.

Dolly Winthrop: She is the simple but kindly wife of the wheelwright, Ben Winthrop, and the mother of Eppie's future husband, Aaron. Dolly's kindness for others is her chief virtue. She befriends Silas, after his discovery of Eppie, and teaches him the proper ways to dress and feed her. Moreover, her missionary spirit results in a return to religion for Silas. Optimistic, patient, altruistic, and religious, her strongest concern and best talent is for helping others when they are in distress.

ESSAY QUESTIONS AND ANSWERS

1. What is the theme of the novel?

ANSWER: In *Silas Marner,* the purpose which George Eliot had in writing the work was to show how natural, human influences could remedy a damaged personality. This remedial effect which human affection creates was one of the ideas she borrowed from the Romantic poet, William Wordsworth. He expressed the thought that a child, more than any other thing which an aging man may love, brings with it "hope and forward looking thoughts." Silas Marner is returned to hopeful life through the love he gives and receives from the child, Eppie.

2. Why is there a double metamorphosis in Silas Marner?

ANSWER: The first metamorphosis or change in Silas occurs in Lantern Yard. He loses his faith in God and his fellow human beings when he is "framed" unjustly by William Dane and then found guilty through the superstitious irrational method of choosing lots. Comparing him to a spider, the author shows him working at his loom; content to live a lone existence in which a love of gold has replaced human and divine love. The second great change in Silas occurs fifteen years after his arrival in Raveloe. The loss of his gold and the discovery of Eppie force him to seek assistance from his neighbors. They begin to express interest in him and the child; many of them become anxious to help. The presence of the child in his home rekindles Silas' love which his experience at Lantern Yard had extinguished long ago. A second transformation occurs as Silas returns slowly to his original belief and hope in God and man.

3. What are the major strengths and weaknesses of the novel?

ANSWER: Foremost, perhaps, of the major attributes of *Silas Marner* is the realistic picture it leaves of nineteenth-century English country life. Other considerations include:

(1) An ingenious and complex double plot structure in which the stories of the two protagonists, Godfrey and Silas, are balanced without mere imitation. Both are deceived by unscrupulous men: one a friend, the other a brother. Their separate stories are united twice by incidents which force them to make decisions of far-reaching effect. When Eppie is found on his doorstep, Silas decides to keep her; Godfrey chooses to ignore his responsibility to her so that he may marry Nancy. Fourteen years later, the discovery of Dunstan Cass' skeleton prompts Godfrey to reveal his relationship to the child. (See diagram for outline of the plot.)

(2) The characterizations of Silas, Godfrey Cass, Nancy, Dunsey, the Squire, Priscilla, and the gallery of village types in early nineteenth-century England is credible throughout the work.

(3) The ethical considerations in the novel are many and are clearly underlined. The value of a novel as a work of art is, to some, dependent upon the lessons it teaches. The ideas *Silas Marner* touches are handled from a decidedly didactic viewpoint; the author, in her closings, often repeats the obvious interpretation suggested earlier.

Perhaps the most frequent adverse criticsm of the novel is its excessive moralizing by the narrator. The explicit homilies, which many consider valuable for their teaching, are viewed by others as little more than superfluous sermonettes. In addition, certain of the scenes, such as Molly Farren trudging through the snow-covered lanes in the gloom or the renunciation of Godfrey by his child may appear, to today's readers, quaintly archaic or maudlin.

4 **What is the general plot structure of the novel?**

ANSWER: There are two stories: one is of Silas Marner; the other is of Godfrey Cass. Their lives intersect three times. See A, B, and C.

Silas is born.

Silas is 24; he is found guilty of robbery at Lantern Yard.	Godfrey is born.
Silas is 39 and has lived in Raveloe for fifteen years.	Godfrey is 24; he marries Molly Farren; Eppie is born.

A. November: Theft of gold by Dunsey Cass.

B. December: Finding of Eppie in the snow.
Molly Farren dies.

Silas rears Eppie.	Godfrey marries Nancy. He refuses to recognize Eppie as his child.

C. Silas is 55; Godfrey is 40.
The body of Dunstan Cass is found.
Godfrey tells Nancy of his marriage and child.
Silas and Eppie refuse to part.

Wedding of Eppie.

DETAILED SUMMARY OF MIDDLEMARCH A STUDY OF PROVINCIAL LIFE

PRELUDE

Years ago Saint Teresa, as a little girl, went with her younger brother out into the world to do good; until her uncles stopped them. However, her epic life was not to be denied her; later, she reformed a religious order. This Spanish woman was not the last of her kind: many young girls with gifts of heart and mind are born but, because of adversity or mistakes, they live a simple, mean, or unheralded life. Such women are the foundresses of nothing and they spend their good-intentioned lives without accomplishing anything; their energies never overcome the hindrances which life presents.

COMMENT: For the sake of clarity, George Eliot uses the brief prelude (or introduction) to state her theme: the forgotten women in life never realize their greatness because of their inability to remove obstacles of fortune and situation from their lives. The novel is perhaps more important, however, as a realistic picture of English life on various social levels in the time of the passing of the reform bill in England (1832). This was a law which gave the right to vote to thousands who never had it; thus changing England into a more democratic society.

BOOK ONE: MISS BROOKE, CHAPTER ONE

The time is 1829; the place is Tipton Grange, a village in England. As the novel opens, we are introduced to two sisters, Dorothea and Cecelia Brooke. The older sister, Dorothea, is only nineteen but she is extremely mature and serious. Her sister, although not very much younger, is more concerned with clothes and jewelry. Their parents are dead; both girls live with their uncle, an unpredictable man of sixty. We find that Dorothea wishes to devote her life to doing "good"; to associating herself with some great man. She divides her dead mother's jewels with Cecelia but she feels guilty because she retains even one for herself. Celia is hurt by her domineering but kindly sister; judging that Dorothea (if she really believed that the jewels were of little value) should not have taken any of them. The sisters are expecting two men for dinner that evening: Sir James Chettam, Dorothea's suitor, and Rev. Edward Casaubon, a scholar of some reputation who is engaged in writing a long research work.

BOOK ONE, CHAPTER TWO

That evening at dinner, Dorothea expresses a dislike for horseback riding. This disappoints Sir James but Rev. Casaubon defends her right to give up certain pleasures if she wishes. Dorothea is evidently pleased by this remark; Celia senses that she is interested in their new friend even though he is "towards fifty" and has a sallow complexion and "two white moles with hairs on them." Sir James, rebuffed by Dorothea, begins to find interest in Celia who is much more "agreeable as well as pretty" than her sister.

BOOK ONE, CHAPTER THREE

The next morning, Dorothea continues her conversation with Rev. Casaubon, rector of Lowick. She is thrilled to be with such a brilliant man. His work is to be *A Key to All Mythologies*: the man's natural beliefs are identical with supernatural truths. Later, Dorothea dreams of becoming his wife and secretary. She romantically imagines herself as a sharer in his great goal: the completion of his book. A few days later, she meets Sir James; he agrees to help her with her own favorite idea: the construction of cottages for the poor of the village. She becomes more tolerant of him and, although he may interpret this new warmth as a fondness for him, Dorothea still sees him only as a possible husband for Celia. Casaubon now becomes a continual visitor and Dorothea, mentioning her plans for cottages, is disappointed to find he is not interested. She accepts his rebuff assuming that he is too busy with his book. If she were married to him, she reasons, she could still have the cottage program as other women have hobbies to occupy themselves. This would be when she is not functioning as secretary for him.

BOOK ONE, CHAPTER FOUR

Dorothea discovers, from Celia, that Sir James is in love with her and not her younger sister. Her revulsion is so great that tears well up in her eyes. She tells Celia that she has been "barely polite" to him. She is also upset when she discovers that the villagers do not consider her cottage plans very highly. They call it a "fad." She becomes angry and looks on Celia as a "thorn in her spirit." Later, her uncle (Mr. Brooke) tells her that Rev. Casaubon has a very high opinion of her. Finally, she tells of his offer of marriage. He is unaware of how much she cares for him and her interest surprises him. (She says she is "honored.") He proceeds to remind her of the disadvantages of such a marriage. Casaubon is almost fifty; Dorothea is nineteen. Yet Mr. Brooke recognizes that Casaubon's scholarly ways may suit her.

BOOK ONE, CHAPTER FIVE

The chapter opens with a letter which Rev. Casaubon has written as marriage proposal to Dorothea. He gives an "accurate statement" of his feelings in inflated, pedantic prose. Dorothea, however, feels that a whole new life is opening for her; she answers him immediately, seeing no reason to defer her reply. She tells him she is grateful to him and looks forward to their marriage. Her uncle advises her to be cautious and to delay the marriage but Rev. Casaubon is invited to dinner. Dorothea's excitement is sensed by Celia who proceeds to ridicule the rector until Dorothea finally reveals her engagement to him. Celia is amazed; the idea of such a marriage is incomprehensible to her. However, after dinner, Dorothea and Rev. Casaubon, who speaks (with "frigid rhetoric") of their relationship, find themselves happy together and decide to marry within six weeks.

> **COMMENT:** Immediately we sense that the motives of Dorothea and the rector are unusual for people in love. He wishes to have a wife who will fill up the lonely periods in his life when he is not studying; she always wished to devote herself to a noble cause and now she has her chance. She can become wife and secretary to a scholar involved in important research.

BOOK ONE, CHAPTER SIX

Mrs. Cadwallader, wife of the rector of Tipton and Freshitt, arrives at Mr. Brooke's house as Rector Casaubon is leaving. She is a "match-maker," interested in advancing the hopes of Sir James for Dorothea. Mr. Brooke avoids the uncomfortable task of breaking the news to her about the match; leaving this to Celia. Mrs. Cadwallader is dismayed. "Frightful," she remarks before leaving to inform Sir James. His reaction is similar: "Horrible." However, Mrs. Cadwallader suggests that he is indeed well rid of Dorothea; Celia is the better choice of the two. Sir James finds himself agreeing when he next goes to visit at the Grange.

BOOK ONE, CHAPTER SEVEN

Rev. Casaubon visits Dorothea continually in the time prior to their marriage. She accepts willingly the role of disciple; asking him to teach her Latin and Greek so that she may be of greater assistance to him and, also, to develop her range of knowledge. Her stuffy uncle objects; he tells her that such deep studies as the classics and mathematics are too taxing for any woman. Dorothea would be better employed studying music. Mr. Brooke views Casaubon as being affluent and a sensible person; perhaps, one day he might even become a dean or a bishop.

BOOK ONE, CHAPTER EIGHT

In this chapter, we are concerned primarily with Sir James' attempts to prevent the match. Shocked by a belief that Dorothea is infatuated with the scholarly manner of the rector, he is convinced that Mr. Brooke should have prevented the match. He visits Rector Cadwallader and asks him to intervene on the grounds that Dorothea is not of age. The rector, however, sees no harm in the match if Dorothea loves Casaubon although he admits that his fellow clergyman has a "dry" kind of personality. Mrs. Cadwallader now enters and tells Sir James that she and her husband have "washed their hands" concerning the marriage. Sir James decides to continue his plans for the cottages that Dorothea desired; he now finds himself deriving pleasure from Celia's company.

BOOK ONE, CHAPTER NINE

Dorothea *must* see her future home so she travels to Lowick with her sister and uncle. The flower beds need tending; the house is old-English style, small-windowed and melancholy-looking but it could be cheery with the addition of children, open windows and flowers. Celia is disappointed, but Dorothea feels that the house is "hollowed" and wants it left the same. They meet Mr. Tucker, the curate, who answers all of Dorothea's questions; she is disappointed that the people of the village appear well and satisfied and that there is nothing she can do. At the house again, Rev. Casaubon introduces his second cousin, Will Ladislaw, an artist. He has decided that anyone marrying Rev. Casaubon must be unpleasant; a woman who could not laugh or have passion. Rev. Casaubon has decided to send him to Italy to study; thereby letting him test his freedom. He hopes that he will turn out well.

BOOK ONE, CHAPTER TEN

Will decides not to fix his European destination any more precisely than the "Continent." Rev. Casaubon still feels surprised at his forthcoming marriage to Dorothea. She looks forward to marriage as opening new vistas of learning for her. They decide they shall visit Rome on their wedding trip and he is disappointed that Celia will not be able to accompany Dorothea as a companion. They plan a dinner party at the Grange, the last preliminary preparation for the wedding. Dorothea is the subject of many observations of the townspeople at the party. The women think she is too "earnest." They speak of Lydgate, the new doctor, and see similarities between Dorothea and Rosamond Vincy (the ambitious daughter of the mayor). Soon after the party, the marriage takes place and the Rector and Mrs. Casaubon leave for Rome on their honeymoon.

COMMENT: In this chapter, George Eliot introduces a new plot and new characters: Dr. Lydgate and Rosamond Vincy. They will be our chief concern for the next eight chapters.

BOOK ONE, CHAPTER ELEVEN

Dr. Lydgate is attracted to Rosamond Vincy, a pretty, well-educated girl from a fine family. He feels that he should not marry, however, until he establishes himself. Miss Vincy is tired of the same provincial faces and wishes her father would introduce her to Lydgate. Her brother, Fred, informs her that their uncle, Peter Featherstone, is ill and that he is going to visit him when Dr. Lydgate goes to attend him. Rosamond feels that this would be an opportunity to meet the new doctor and she decides to go along.

BOOK ONE, CHAPTER TWELVE

The wealthy Peter Featherstone is very seriously ill and is visited by his sister, Mrs. Waule, at Stone Court in Lowick. She suggests to him that Fred Vincy, his nephew, has borrowed a good deal of money (160 pounds or the equivalent of more than 3,000 dollars) on the belief that Peter will soon die and leave him an inheritance. When Fred and Rosamond arrive, Peter speaks alone to his nephew; informing him of what he has just heard. Fred, denying the rumor, agrees to bring a letter from Mr. Bulstrode, the banker, vindicating him of the charge of borrowing on his uncle's will. Peter implies that he may help Fred pay his debts if he receives such a letter. Meanwhile, Rosamond receives a thumb-nail sketch of Dr. Lydgate from Peter's housekeeper, Mary Garth. She is a plain girl of twenty-two who is interested in Fred.

Dr. Lydgate arrives for his daily visit to the patient and he and Rosamond find that they enjoy each other's company. She is pleased to see that he is interested in her (as she had expected). On her way home she has reveries that he is in love with her; her brother Fred is meditating on his visit with his uncle, hoping that his father will take upon himself the unpleasant task of speaking to Bulstrode.

BOOK TWO: OLD AND YOUNG, CHAPTER THIRTEEN

Mr. Bulstrode, the banker, is visited by Dr. Lydgate; Bulstrode wants to become superintendent of the new hospital that he is building in Middlemach. Bulstrode shows his political sense by suggesting that Lydgate support Mr. Tyke over Mr. Farebrother as his choice for chaplain of the old infirmary. As he leaves, Lydgate meets Mr. Vincy, Fred's father, and accepts a dinner invitation from him.

After an uncomfortable beginning, the conversation between Mr. Vincy and Bulstrode about the letter appears successful. Bulstrode promises to consult his wife (Vincy's sister) before making a decision although he feels that Vincy may be taking advantage of his sister's influence.

BOOK TWO, CHAPTER FOURTEEN

The next day, Bulstrode writes the letter to Peter Featherstone who finally agrees to give Fred one hundred pounds. This is sixty pounds less than he needs to pay his debts. Fred seeks out Mary Garth who taunts him for his irresponsibility and debts. Fred is interested in marrying Mary but she will make no promises to a man who would not be accepted by her father. She asks him "never to speak to her that way again." Fred is chagrined because it is Mary's father who is the signer of the bill which Fred owes to his creditor.

BOOK TWO, CHAPTER FIFTEEN

This chapter gives background material about Dr. Lydgate. We see that he was one of three orphaned children; at a young age he became interested in anatomy and in dedicating himself to medicine. At twenty-seven, he became involved with an actress in Paris, and offered to marry her through "impetuous folly" after she had been accused of killing her husband. To his sorrow, Lydgate discovered that she had killed him out of hate and not by chance as he had believed. Disillusioned with women and determined to remain aloof, he decided to settle down to a life of service and research in Middlemarch.

> **COMMENT:** George Eliot digresses in the opening paragraph of this chapter to tell us that she must advance the novel quickly. "I have so much to do in unravelling certain human lots and seeing how they were woven and interwoven." Here, we see one of the chief aspects of her skill as a novelist: the ability to construct believable and interesting plots. Her plans are complex and complete; she ties up her separate stories with great skill. (Compare this with the plot sequences in *Salis Marner*.)

BOOK TWO, CHAPTER SIXTEEN

The question of appointing Mr. Tyke as hospital chaplain is an interesting topic to the people of Middlemach. It indicates the power of the banker, Mr. Bulstrode; he knows the financial secrets of most traders of the town, for he administers the town charities. He wants to use his power for the "glory of God" but he has gone through much "spiritual conflict."

Mr. Vincy believes that Mr. Farebrother should be chaplain as the hospital is in his parish. Lydgate believes reforms would be affected by Mr. Tyke. He and Rosamond become engrossed in conversation; he finds her attractive and accomplished. He leaves at eleven o'clock after judging that he will be unable to marry for several years: "therefore he was not ready to entertain the notion of being in love with a girl he happened to admire." He decides to look into Lewis' new book on *Fever*. It did not occur to Lydgate that he has been the subject of eager meditation for Rosamond; who sees no reason to delay her marriage.

BOOK TWO, CHAPTER SEVENTEEN

Lydgate is invited to dine at the home of Mr. Farebrother. The house is old and dated. He lives with his mother (still under seventy); her sister, Miss Noble; and Miss Winifred Farebrother, the Vicar's older sister. His mother "was evidently accustomed to tell her company what they ought to think, and to regard no subject as quite safe without her steering." She informs Lydgate that they are not often in want of medical aid as she is very careful in rearing her children.

Mr. Farebrother shows Dr. Lydgate his collection of nature study specimens. Lydgate senses that this man of the cloth may have desired a different vocation. (Perhaps, the dominance of his mother was responsible for his choice of the ministry over nature study.) Mr. Farebrother, who has acute insight into human motives and acts, suggests that Lydgate avail himself of Bulstrode's favor and asistance by voting for Mr. Tyke as chaplain. He confides to Lydgate that they should remain friends regardless of how he votes.

BOOK TWO, CHAPTER EIGHTEEN

Lydgate is developing a friendship with Rev. Farebrother. Farebrother's character and conduct are unusually fine; his sermons are delivered without notes and people outside his parish come to hear him. At Mr. Bulstrode's request, Lydgate is laying plans for the interior of the hospital. The Vicar is known to play at billiards and has been seen in the Green Dragon; the local tavern. Lydgate thinks that a vote for Tyke would make him a vassal of Bulstrode's but he is afraid, if Farebrother receives the chaplaincy, the extra forty pounds he receives would be used for cards. What Lydgate really cares for, however, is his work and the hospital.

Lydgate remains uncertain whether Tyke is the proper man for the chaplaincy. He arrives late the night of the voting and is forced to give the tie-breaking vote. He chooses Mr. Tyke (who is Bustrode's choice) but he feels uneasy afterwards.

BOOK TWO, CHAPTER NINETEEN

In this chapter, we return ot the story of Dorothea and her husband, the rector. Will Ladislaw, traveling in Rome, learns from a German artist (Adolf Naumann) that Dorothea is in Rome. His friend describes his reaction to her beauty as he saw her admiring the statuary in the Vatican; adding that he is very desirous of having this "madonna" pose for him. Ladislaw refuses to help his friend win her consent to have her portrait painted; even though her husband is his relative. Naumann suggests the possibility of jealousy which Ladislaw rejects openly. Yet, he does have certain misgivings about his motives; why did he object so strenously to his friend's proposed portrait of her?

BOOK TWO, CHAPTER TWENTY

In this chapter, we return to the story of Dorothea and her husband, terly." She is melancholic and attempts to determine the causes of her grief. It is primarily the result of disappointment:

(1) Present day Rome (1829) has lost much of the idealized beauty she had imagined its proud past to have displayed.

(2) She is aware that her new husband is less of a warm human being and more of a cold, disciplined note-taker than she had imagined.

COMMENT: The differences between appearances and reality are one of the chief topics of writers. Here, we notice how the truth of her mistake is made known to Dorothea after a few weeks of marriage. The rector is also disappointed. Expecting to have won a docile secretary, he is furious to hear Dorothea suggest that she will help him only if he actually begins to write the work. The power of George Eliot to suggest the psychological is evident in this chapter.

BOOK TWO, CHAPTER TWENTY-ONE

Hurriedly drying her tears, Dorothea opens the door of the apartment to a visitor, Will Ladislaw. Casaubon is doing further research at the Vatican Library. Privately, Will is annoyed with his cousin for leaving his new bride at home, alone, while he pursues his insignificant details elsewhere. Dorothea, although she has just been reminiscing about her husband's tutorial manner and lack of warmth, speaks glowingly about his studies. Much to her consternation, Will suggests that Casaubon's labors may be unnecessary because of the strides in research now being made by German historians. Casaubon returns: ending the conversation. Then, he invites Will to dinner the following evening although he senses displeasure in discovering him as a visitor. After he leaves, he receives an apology from Dorothea for her upsetting conduct at breakfast.

COMMENT: It is significant to note that Dorothea learns to adjust herself to Casaubon; although she is aware of his faults, she feels herself obliged to consider his feelings, also.

BOOK TWO, CHAPTER TWENTY-TWO

The next evening at dinner, all is pleasant: the displeasure the rector has experienced with his cousin's presence has been mollified and Will is ingratiantingly agreeable company. Dorothea and her husband even accept an invitation to accompany Will on a tour of artist studios for the following day.

When they visit Naumann's studio, the artist, who is painting a full canvas of the Saints of the Church, asks Casaubon to pose for the head of St. Thomas Aquinas. He is obviously flattered and consents to return. Dorothea is also persuaded to return for a pencil sketch; but, Neumann's rhapsodizing of her beauty is becoming increasingly more irritating to Will.

Before leaving Rome, Will pays a last visit to the Casaubons' apartment when Dorothea is again alone. In their discussion of her husband's career, Dorothea expresses her thoughts about his efforts and their possible failure. She admits that he may be working for nought but defends his right to labor in vain. To fail grandly is better than never to have made an attempt. Will, now concurring with this view, reveals his plan to abandon his benefactor's (Casaubon) generosity by returning to England to become independent. He leaves Dorothea later. She tells her husband of Will's new determination but he is only interested listlessly. At his request, Dorothea does not mention Will's name again.

BOOK THREE, CHAPTER TWENTY-THREE

Fred Vincy is troubled owing money to Mr. Bambridge, a horse dealer, because it is understood that his "company was much sought in Middlemarch by young men understood to be 'addicted to pleasure'." Fred feels that he should begin to consider the limits of his father's money. He chooses to ask his friends for money but eliminates all but the "poorest and kindest," Caleb Garth.

Mr. Garth has a high opinion of Fred; he is sure the lad will turn out well, so when Fred's debt is three months overdue, Caleb signs the note for him. Fred feels that he must repay the note as soon as possible so that Caleb will not lower his opinion of him.

He goes to the horse fair hoping to sell his horse and make some money to pay off the note. He has eighty pounds left from the hundred given him by Peter Featherstone. He sees a horse which he hopes to sell to Lord Medlicote for eighty pounds so he trades his own horse and thirty pounds for the new horse. As he returns home, he has one hundred and thirty pounds.

BOOK THREE, CHAPTER TWENTY-FOUR

Diamond, the horse Fred has bought and for which he hopes to receive eighty pounds when he sells it to Lord Medlicate, turns out to be very vicious, and Fred blames himself when he catches his foot on a rope. Fred is very downcast since the horse is now worthless. He sees Mrs. Garth who has a "motherly feeling" toward him; however, she probably would not have been happy if her daughter Mary had become engaged to Fred. She is teaching grammer and baking pies for her younger children when Fred arrives. He explains to Caleb Garth that he cannot ask his father for the remainder of the money for it would be useless to do so. He has only fifty pounds left to give to Mr. Garth. He and his wife discuss their plight. They decide that the only solution is to get together as much of their savings as they have, and to make up the remaining money due on the note which he had signed for Fred. Caleb realizes now how foolish he had been because he must pay the money out of his meager savings. He also realizes that he will have to ask Mary, his daughter, to give them some of her money because they are able to find only ninety-two pounds and are short twenty-four.

BOOK THREE, CHAPTER TWENTY-FIVE

Fred wants to visit Mary before Caleb arrives to tell her that she will have to give him part of her savings. This is to make up the remainder of the debt owed by Fred. She is at Stone Court. Fred is remorseful: "I am a good-for-nothing blackguard." Mary begins to cry when he tells her about the debt. When he begs for forgiveness she asks him candidly, if he thinks forgiveness could restore the lost money. She calls him selfish, then tells him that he gets into trouble through his "idle pleasures." When he seems distraught, she begins to pity him. He promises: "I will try to be anything you like, Mary, if you say you will love me."

When Caleb arrives, she gives him twenty-four pounds; although he needs only eighteen. He cautions her against Fred and she replies that she "will never engage herself to one who has no manly independence, and who goes on loitering away his time on the chance that others will provide for him."

BOOK THREE, CHAPTER TWENTY-SIX

Fred becomes ill and his mother calls for Doctor Wrench (a small neat bilious man, with a well-dressed wig) who tells him he has a "slight derangement." He becomes sicker, however, when he tries to carry on his daily routine. They are not able to reach Dr. Wrench. Freds' sister, Rosamond, sees Dr. Lydgate out of the window and tells her mother to call him. (She heard that he was a good doctor who cured Ellen Bulstrode.) Lydgate thinks Fred has typhoid fever and prescribes various treatments including complete bedrest. When Mr. Vincy hears of Lydgates diagnosis, he is angry with Wrench for his incorrect diagnosis. Lydgate becomes the Vincys' family doctor amid much town gossip about the medical error.

BOOK THREE, CHAPTER TWENTY-SEVEN

Fred is delirious and Mrs. Vincy cries to Lydgate to "save him." Fred's illness presents great opportunities for Rosamond to talk to Lydgate. She is with him a great deal because Mrs. Vincy never leaves Fred's side. Lydgate finds it more and more agreeable to be with her and he feels that a flirtation would be harmless. However, he has made an enemy in Mr. Ned Plymdale (who was considered one of the good matches in Middlemarch). He is jealous of Rosamond's time with Lydgate. Rosamond fels that she and Lydgate are as good as engaged; he, however, still seems to be more interested in his study of primitive tissue.

BOOK THREE, CHAPTER TWENTY-EIGHT

Rev. and Mrs. Casaubon return home to Lowick Manor in the middle of January. The rooms in the house and the furnishing seem to have shrunk. One morning, while Rev. Casaubon is in his library with his curate, Mr. Tucker, Mr. Brooke comes to visit with Celia. He repeats to Dorothea that Casaubon appears "a little pale." Celia's blushing finally leads to her revelation that she and Sir James are to be married. Dorothea is pleased.

> **COMMENT**· Notice how Eliot uses images in the room's physical setting to evoke a mood. Dorothea's reaction to the house is that it seems smaller and more confining. This suggests that her hopes for success and happiness in her marriage have also shunk.

BOOK THREE, CHAPTER TWENTY-NINE

The chapter begins with an analysis of Rev. Casaubon's thoughts about his marriage. He has viewed Dorothea as a good potential secretary-wife; never considering her rights to happiness in marriage. Now, he holds great misgivings about his own powers as a scholar and has never really experienced the joy of life. His chief and nervous concern is the egotistical preservation of a reputation for brilliance.

Rev. Casaubon has received a two-page letter from Will for Dorothea.

As he gives it to her, he remarks that he hopes that she does not want Will to visit them for he has no "leisure" to waste upon "desultory vivacity." Dorothea is shocked and angry that he prejudges her and so underestimates her concern for his privacy. Thirty minutes later, Casaubon suffers an attack, just as Celia and Sir James arrive. They dispatch a servant to Dr. Lydgate immediately.

BOOK THREE, CHAPTER THIRTY

Casaubon's attack is not fatal. Dr. Lydgate advises Dorothea that he could live for fifteen years or that he could die, suddenly. He is not to be informed of these possibilities because of the anxiety it might cause him. Above all else, he must avoid consternation. Dorothea asks her uncle to write to Will asking him to forgo any visit to Lowick because of her husband's illness. As Mr. Brooke is writing the letter, he suddenly decides to invite Will to his home but he fails to reveal the invitation to Dorothea.

BOOK THREE, CHAPTER THIRTY-ONE

Mrs. Bulstrode has been making frequent visits to Middlemarch, primarily to arrange a match between Ned Plymdale and her niece, Rosamond. However, Mrs. Plymdale mentions that she believes that there is something between Rosamond and Dr. Lydgate. Mrs. Bulstrode appears shocked and confronts Rosamond with the news. Rosamond is embarrased but ttells her that, although there is nothing "definite" between her and Lydgate, she could feel nothing towards Ned Plymdale. Because Rosamond will not tell her anything, Mrs. Bulstrode feels it is her duty to arrange a meeting with Lydgate to question his intentions. She tells him that he should not take up so much of her time unless he intends to marry her.

Because of this advice, Lydgate visits the Vincy household only when necessary. Rosamond does not know his reasons for neglecting her and is, therefore, very cold to him when he makes a visit. She involuntarily begins to cry; Lydgate suddenly realizes that he does love her and wishes to marry her. They seek out Mr. Vincy who gives his consent at once.

BOOK THREE, CHAPTER THIRTY-TWO

All of Peter Featherstone's greedy relatives become interested in his will when they realize that he is close to death. They come to his house but he does not wish to see any of them. However, his brother and sister, Solomon and Jane, refuse to comply with his requests and go into his room. They are very upset to see Mrs. Vincy and Fred for fear that these two may have encouraged their brother to change his will in their favor.

Featherstone's cousin, Borthrup Trumbull (who is also his business advisor) takes a fancy to Mary Garth, Peter's housekeeper, in the hope that his cousin may find it in his heart to be kind to her in his will. Of it, Solomon says, "You may depend my brother has left that girl a lumping sum."

BOOK THREE, CHAPTER THIRTY-THREE

That night, after midnight, while Mary is sitting up with Featherstone, she thinks how ridiculous his relatives are in pretending to be interested in his welfare. About three o'clock, Featherstone calls her to his side and asks her how many of his relatives are in the house. He tells her that they are all fools; that he is in full possession of his faculties and knows what they are up to. He says that he has had two wills drawn up and wants to burn out of them. She does not wish to be open to suspicion by helping him to do this so he tells her to call Fred Vincy. She urges him to call a lawyer but he refuses. He orders her to open the chest and take out money in the box. (No one knows that it is there.) She refuses again and, in anger, he throws a stick at her, but it falls to the floor. It is getting toward morning; she puts more wood on the fading fire. Peter Featherstone is dead before morning arrives.

BOOK FOUR: THREE LOVE PROBLEMS, CHAPTER THIRTY-FOUR

Peter Featherstone is buried on a cloudy and chilly morning in May. The news has spread that Featherstone left written directions for a "big burying", for a funeral "beyond his betters." He loved money and loved spend it in gratification of his own peculiar tastes. The three mourning coaches are met by the clergyman, Mr. Cadwallader. His wife, Mrs. Cadwallader, watches the funeral from an upper window in their house at Lowick. She is with Celia and Sir James Chettam. They discuss the various people attending the funeral and notice a man with whom they are not familiar. They describe him as having "a little round head with bulging eyes—a sort of frog-face." They have never seen him before.

Mr. Brooke enters and tells them of his guest, Will Ladislaw. Dorothea and Mr. Casaubon (also watching the funeral) are noticeably disturbed by the news but Mr. Brooke is apparently unaware of their feelings, for he speaks glowingly of Will's future.

BOOK FOUR, CHAPTER THIRTY-FIVE

George Eliot compares the gathering of relatives for the reading of Peter Featherstone's will to the animals which gathered on Noah's Ark to "feed on the same store of fodder." Even in their greedy anxiety, however, they are concerned with the identity of the "frog-faced" man.

Mr. Standish, the lawyer, expected to read the last of three wills he had drawn up for Mr. Featherstone. He is surprised to find two wills. The will dated August 9, 1825, left ten thousand pounds to Fred Vincy; and land and property were to be given to the "frog-faced" man, whose name is Joshua Rigg. He was to be the sole executor and was to take the name of Featherstone. His greedy relatives were to receive only small sums. They are all shocked and demand that Mr. Standish read the second will. This will revoked the bequests to all but Riggs, who was to receive "all the land lying in Lowick parish, with all the stock and household furniture." The remainder was to be used for the construction of Featherstone's Alms-Houses for old men.

> **COMMENT**: Disappointed and indignant, all of Featherstone's relatives speak of their true dislike for him. Fred feels ill from the reading of the will, for Featherstone's second will was probably written to punish Fred for borrowing money.

BOOK FOUR, CHAPTER THIRTY-SIX

The reading of the will makes Mr. Vincy angry and he now regards Fred's idleness with more severity. He tells him that he must return to school and pass his examination. Fred is too depressed to make any objections. Still in bad humor, Mr. Vincy tells his wife he refuses to give his consent for Rosamond to marry Lydgate because he thinks he "hasn't a farthing."

Rosamond does not believe that her father means what he says and Lydgate continues to spend most of his evenings at their home. He thinks that it would be best to marry within half a year as "this unsettled state of affairs uses up the time." A married man can devote more time to his work. Rosamond finally reveals her father's objections to Lydgate and he tells her that, if she is unhappy at home, they should hasten their marriage. They agree on a date six weeks hence and begin to make plans for their home and for their wedding journey.

BOOK FOUR, CHAPTER THIRTY-SEVEN

In the beginning of this chapter, George Eliot discusses the political situation of the times; there is a cry for reform of existing conditions. Mr. Brooke secretly bought the *Pioneer,* a newspaper in Middlemach and he wrote a brilliant article in it which was edited by Will Ladislaw. Mr. Broke's interest in politics began as a youth but his family and friends are now opposed both to his idea of entering public life and to Will Ladislaw.

Will is anxious to work on the newspaper; he goes to see Dorothea not only to ask advice, but to see her as well. Mr. Casaubon has gone to see the Archedeacon; Dorothea is alone. He tells her of the offer and she later tells her husband of Will's visit. He shows much displeasure. Later that evening, he writes a letter to Will expressing his objections to Will's taking a job with Mr. Brooke.

Because Dorothea spends so much time alone, she has time to think of the family's poor treatment of Will's grandmother. She was cut off from the family inheritance and from family protection because her family did not approve of the man she married. Dorothea thinks this situation should be righted, and she mentions it to her husband; suggesting that he make provision in his will to give his cousin Will half of his estate. Rev. Casaubon becomes enraged and forbids Dorothea to mention this matter again.

The following day, Rev. Casaubon receives a reply from Will who tells him that he intends to take the job with Mr. Brooke, regardless of the objections of his benefactor. Casaubon is filled with disgust and suspicion but can turn to no one for advice because he is distrustful of everyone's feelings toward him. He remains silent.

BOOK FOUR, CHAPTER THIRTY-EIGHT

Sir James Chettam is dissatisfied with Mr. Brooke's interest in politics. He goes to visit the Cadwalladers because discussion upsets Celia. They all believe that Mr. Brooke's campaign will result in failure. Rumors are that Ladislaw is "a quill-driving alien, a foreign emissary, and what not." In discussing the good and bad points of Mr. Brooke's decision, Mr. Cadwallader thinks that a loss might make him more conscious of the management of his estate. Sir James thinks that the management of his estate would be improved only if he were to re-hire Caleb Garth, whom he had fired twelve years earlier.

Mr. Brooke enters and they discuss with him the highly critical article written about him in the town's rival newspaper, *The Trumpet*. Mr. Brooke believes that the people in Middlemarch are backward and need to be educated. They all agree that, if a man decides to enter public life, he must be willing to accept the consequences which aften are in the form of ridicule and expense.

BOOK FOUR, CHAPTER THIRTY-NINE

Sir James thinks that Dorothea could have influence in trying to dissuade her uncle against entering politics and also in persuading him to make reforms in the management of his estate. He arranges for her to meet him at the Grange. Mr. Brooke tells her that he hopes she is not getting too learned for a woman. She "pours forth" her emotions, telling him of how he might make vast improvements in his estate. He is stunned to realize how much help she could be but he decides to ignore her advice.

Will Ladislaw takes this opportunity to tell Dorothea of his correspondence with Rev. Casaubon, who forbade him to visit his home again. Dorothea feels wretched and thinks her husband is completely wrong.

After his visit with Dorothea, Mr. Brooke finds it necessary to make an infrequent visit to one of his tenants; a man named Dagley. The man speaks loudly and disrespectfully to Mr. Brooke who is astonished to find that he is not as popular a landlord as he had believed.

BOOK FOUR, CHAPTER FORTY

This chapter tells us of Caleb Garth and his family. Mary Garth must look for a new position after the death of Peter Featherstone. She has decided to go to York to teach although she is not fond of schoolrooms. While they are eating breakfast, Caleb opens a letter he has received from Sir James, requesting that he manage Brooke's estates. It will be a position with more than adequate pay; Mary will not have to leave. His wife considers the offer a blessing.

The vicar, Mr. Farebrother, pays a visit to the family that evening. He wishes to see not only Caleb and his wife but Mary, also. He tells them that he has come as an envoy of Fred Vincy who has been out of town at school for many months. The vicar remarks that Fred is trying again for his degree but the couple feels that he should not enter the church.

After hearing this information, Caleb seems to be ready to give Fred another chance to prove himself as manager of the estate but his wife is not so ready to agree to such an idea.

BOOK FOUR, CHAPTER FORTY-ONE

The transactions between Mr. Bulstrode and Mr. Joshua Rigg Featherstone for the sale of certain property at Stone Court begin. (Notice the name added to Rigg's, as the will required.) Joshua is, as always, "sleek, neat, and cool as the frog he resembled." We meet a new character, Mr. Mr. John Raffles (Rigg's stepfather) who is visiting him. The avaricious Raffles is interested in his step-son's wealth but Joshua remembers Raffles' cruel treatment and neglect of him as a child. He therefore refuses to do more than provide a small weekly dole to Raffles' mother as long as Raffles is alive. He fears that Raffles would take any large sum he might give to her. Raffles leaves; with a paper of Bulstrode's wedged in his leather brandy case. As we shall see, Raffles will want money to keep silent about what he knows of Mr. Bulstrode's past.

BOOK FOUR, CHAPTER FORTY-TWO

Rev. Casaubon requests that Dr. Lydgate reveal to him the whole truth about his illness. He wants to know its nature and his chances for the future. Finally, Lydgate admits that death can be sudden in illnesses such as his. After the doctor's departure, Casaubon rebuffs Dorothea. He secretly envisions her marrying Will after his death. He becomes reconciled with her, however, after spending time alone in the library.

BOOK FIVE: THE DEAD HAND, CHAPTER FORTY-THREE

Dorothea meets Will Ladislaw at the Vincy's home when she goes there to discuss, with Dr. Lydgate, his conversation with Mr. Casaubon. The doctor is absent and she leaves after a brief conversation with Will and Rosamond. They discuss Dorothea in her absence.

Rosamond discovers Will's admiration for Dorothea and, later, she mentions this revelation to her husband.

BOOK FIVE, CHAPTER FORTY-FOUR

Dorothea visits Dr. Lydgate at the New Hospital and learns that no new change has been found in her husband's condition. She also promises two hundred pounds a year to the hospital. Dorothea feels that Lydgate is being treated unjustly by those people who are opposed to him because of Mr. Bulstrode. The doctor admits that he must cooperate with Bulstrode if he is to be practical; he needs money if the projects he plans are ever to become realities.

BOOK FIVE, CHAPTER FORTY-FIVE

The bulk of this chapter shows us, (as the reactions of people to Dr. Lydgate are reported) a cross section of types of nineteenth-century English characters. Mrs. Dappop, the tavern owner, thinks that Lydgate may be guilty of killing people so that he can sell their bodies to medical schools! His conservative colleagues in the medical profession fear his reform policies and their attendant changes.

BOOK FIVE, CHAPTER FORTY-SIX

The new political animation in Middlemarch is apparent with the increased interest in the Reform Bill. Mr. Brooke hopes that the election of a new party will help his chances of winning a seat in Parliament. He and Will Ladislaw discuss what they believe are the most important aspects of the reform and Will becomes a noticeable figure in the town: not only by his editorials but by his speeches. No one in the town knows that he is Casaubon's nephew. Lydgate does not agree with Will on either Mr. Brooke's qualifications or the Reform Bill. Many heated arguments ensue.

Rosamond and Lydgate are expecting a baby and, although he seems to have an avid interest in politics, Lydgate is actually more concerned with his own finances and his inability to pay a furniture bill. Wishing to save Rosamond from worry, however, he remains silent about his money problems.

BOOK FIVE, CHAPTER FORTY-SEVEN

Will sits in his room alone: thinking about his life since he has returned to Middlemarch. He is devoted to Dorothea but he, somehow, enjoys her being "unattainable." He does not wish for Casaubon's death. He seems to enjoy the situation as it now is; he respects and admires her deeply; knowing that she confides in no one as she does in him.

The next morning, he decides to go to Lowick to church, just to see Dorothea; although he knows he will be violating Casaubon's demand that he never visit again. He seems to delight in the prospect of displeasing his cousin. At the church, Will manages only to exchange looks with Dorothea. She looks as if she were repressing tears, probably from embarrassment.

BOOK FIVE, CHAPTER FORTY-EIGHT

Distressed over the disagreement between her husband and Will, Dorothea senses that Will's appearance at church has eliminated any hope for a reconciliation between them. Casaubon, although annoyed about the incident, continues to work diligently on his notebooks. Having difficulty breathing, he decides to rest. That night, he awakens Dorothea to tell her that, in the event of his death, he wants her to carry out his "wishes." She does not give him an answer because she believes that he might expect her to read through the vast amount of notes he has been taking. She continues to ponder his request and, when she finally decides to agree, she goes to tell him in the garden but it is too late to speak to him. Her husband is dead.

BOOK FIVE, CHAPTER FORTY-NINE

Mr. Brooke and Sir. James Chettam discuss Rev. Casaubon's will in the library at Lowick Grange. In a codicil (addition) to the will (in the rage of jealousy) Casaubon had stated that Dorothea was to forfeit the money left to her in the will if she ever married Will Ladislaw. They are shocked by this and decide to protect Dorothea by:

(1) Keeping the contents of the will from her.
(2) "Protecting" her from Ladislaw.

> **COMMENT:** Mr. Brooke is responsible for the second suggestion because he cannot afford to lose Will now that Will has proven himself an able assitant to him in his campaign for Parliament.

BOOK FIVE, CHAPTER FIFTY

Dorothea is visiting her sister Celia and her new baby at Freshitt Hall. She is considering what action to take as the new owner of Lowick Manor. She tells her uncle that she wishes to return to the Manor to go through her husband's papers and to see what plans he may have made regarding the house. He urges her to wait but she is impatient. Inadvertantly, her sister tells her of the secret codicil. Dorothea is shocked because she had never considered Will in the light that Casaubon had presented him. She returns to Lowick Manor to seek any personal message Casaubon may have left for her but, after a thorough search of his papers, she finds nothing.

BOOK FIVE, CHAPTER FIFTY-ONE

Will has not seen Dorothea since the death of Rev. Casaubon. He has been working long hours at the newspaper for the forthcoming election. Before the day of the nomination, Brooke must explain his views to the electors of Middlemach. On his way, he and his friends stop at the Green Dragon and Brooke (normally a non-drinker) takes two glasses of sherry. He begins his speech boldly but, because of the sherry, his ideas begin to slip away rapidly. This is much to the dismay and anger of the crowd.

Will, who had worked strenuously on the campaign, is "thoroughly out of temper" with himself. Brooke decides to withdraw and Will decides to remain in Middlemarch.

BOOK FIVE, CHAPTER FIFTY-TWO

Dorothea asks Rev. Farebrother and his family to be the tenants at Lowick Manor. They are filled with pleasure. His sister suggests to him that now he is in a position to marry and Mary Garth would be a good choice. He advises her that a wife is not to be chosen "as poultry in a market."

A week later, Fred Vincy (who has received his degree from Omnibus College) comes to visit the vicar. He tells him that he does not want to enter the church but he doesn't know what else he might be able to do. He confesses his love for Mary Garth to the vicar. He then asks him to speak to her for him.

Although Farebrother is in love with Mary himself, he goes to her with Fred's request. She tells him that she cannot marry Fred until he proves himself to be a responsible person.

BOOK FIVE, CHAPTER FIFTY-THREE

Joshua Rigg Featherstone sells Stone Court to Mr. Bulstrode; thereby, giving him even more power in Middlemarch. Joshua's real ambition in life is to have a money-changer's shop; he had acquired knowledge of such a career as a child. Peter Featherstone's relatives are happy to see Stone Court in the possession of Bulstrode because they judge the plans of his will to have been disrupted.

On a visit to the land, Mr. Bulstrode encounters Mr. Raffles and recognizes him as an old acquaintance whom he has not seen in twenty-five years. He becomes pale because Raffles knows certain facts about him that even his own wife is unaware of. He gives Raffles two hundred pounds hoping that he will remain silent and stay away. As he leaves, Raffles exclaims "Ladislaw!" evoking a common experience for both Bulstrode and Raffles.

COMMENT: Years earlier, Mr. Bulstrode had married an old, wealthy widow whose daughter was the mother of Will Ladislaw.

BOOK SIX; THE WIDOW AND THE WIFE, CHAPTER FIFTY-FOUR

After Dorothea has been at Freshitt for three months, she becomes increasingly restless; above the objections of Celia, Sir James, and Mrs. Cadwallader she makes plans to return to Lowick. Upon her return, she realizes that her real reason for returning to Lowick Manor is to see Will.

One morning, Will makes a call on her. They both appear uncomfortable but determined in their conversation. He tells her he has come to say goodbye because he is leaving to start a new life in London. She thinks that he must know of the codicil to the will. She then tells him that she will never forget him. Before they are able to say anything else about their true feelings, Sir James enters. Will leaves immediately; after bidding Dorothea goodbye.

BOOK SIX, CHAPTER FIFTY-FIVE

Mrs. Cadwallader, the town matchmaker, sees Dorothea as a possible match for Lord Triton. Her husband cautions her to leave the girl alone. Dorothea's plans are much different, however; never expecting to see Will again, she resolves not to remarry. Her life will be devoted to the organization of a utopian community.

COMMENT: Dorothea is clearly learning to substitute her ideals for simple happiness in love and marriage.

BOOK SIX, CHAPTER FIFTY-SIX

Dorothea's interest in the building of cottages is renewed, especially because of her confidence in Caleb Garth and his approval of her ideas. She finds him to be best suited to manage her land at Lowick Manor.

Railroads are now being built through the smaller towns and villages. They are looked upon by many as being dangerous. The discussion of them is "as exciting a topic as the Reform Bill or the imminent horrors of cholera." One day, Peter Featherstone's brother, Solomon, is responsible for an uprising of tenant farmers against the railroad employees. Caleb Garth is having difficulty calming the angry farmers; just then, Fred Vincy offers to asist him. By coincidence, they both see, in this effort, a chance to improve their relationship; for Fred, in particular, it is a way to prove himself to Mary.

However, he and Caleb are the only members of both families pleased with Fred's job. Mrs. Garth fears that he may never be trustworthy. Mr. Vincy still thinks that Fred should enter the church.

BOOK SIX, CHAPTER FIFTY-SEVEN

That evening, Fred visits Lowick Parsonage to call on Mrs. Garth. He assures her that he can be trusted to do a good job as Caleb's assistant. Even with Fred's reassurance, Mrs. Garth insists that Rev. Farebrother would be a better husband for Mary. Fred fails to realize that Mrs. Garth still looks unfavorably on him; he hopes, after he proves himself, that he will win Mary finally.

BOOK SIX, CHAPTER FIFTY-EIGHT

Captain Lydgate, a cousin of the doctor, pays a visit to the home of Lydgate and Rosamond. He persuades her to go horseback riding; as a result, her baby is born prematurely and dies.

Having incurred numerous bills until he owes a total debt of 380 pounds, Lydgate begins to worry more about his financial situation. Rosamond finally realizes that they are under financial strain; yet, she refuses to change her excessive spending habits. When she suggests that Lydgate ask her father for money, he becomes enraged although he forgives her almost immediately. Sadly, Lydgate looks forward "with dread to the inevitable future discussion about expenditure and the necessity for a complete change in their way of living."

BOOK SIX, CHAPTER FIFTY-NINE

Because gossip in a small town spreads rapidly, it is not long before Rosamond hears of the codicil to Rev. Casaubon's will regarding any marriage between Dorothea and Will. Although warned by Lydgate not to mention it to Will, she reveals it to him. He had not known of it until this time. He calls it a "foul insult" both to Dorothea and to himself and, in anger, tells Rosamond he will never marry Dorothea! Rosamond is concerned both with Will's anger toward her and with Lydgate's financial situation and how it will affect her accustomed way of life.

BOOK SIX, CHAPTER SIXTY

At the end of August, Mr. Bulstrode requests Will to judge the value of a painting he wishes to buy at an auction. Will agrees; using this as an excuse for delaying his departure to London. During the bidding, a red-faced man with whiskers steps in front of Will and asks if his mother's name was Sarah Dunkirk. The stranger, who is Mr. Raffles, appears to have considerable knowledge of Will's family although Will has never seen him before. Raffles tells Will he knew his father and mother. He also reveals to Will that his mother ran away from home when she was a "young lass." Will almost runs away from Raffles in his confusion over the information he has been given about his mother although he knows that there could be nothing dishonorable about her behavior.

COMMENT: An excellent picture of an English country auction is depicted in this chapter. One of the values of this novel is the representation of early nineteenth-century life. The chapter is also a key one in the plot because of Will's conversation with Raffles.

BOOK SIX, CHAPTER SIXTY-ONE

Raffles comes to Mr. Bulstrode's house; when he finds that he is not at home, he leaves abruptly. Realizing that the revelation of his past life will make him the object of scorn in Middlemarch, Bulstrode feels powerless to help himself. In a flashback of memory, he sees himself as a young banker's clerk. He had become close friends with Mr. Dunkirk, the richest man in the congregation of the church. Eventually, he became a confidential accountant in Mr. Dunkirk's pawnbroking business. He soon discovered that the business was receiving stolen goods but he neither made an effort to leave nor to do anything about it. He rationalizes his part in the operation by saying that it was part of a Divine plan. Years later, both Mr. Dunkirk and his only son died, leaving Mrs. Dunkirk alone except for a daughter who ran away from home to go on the stage. This was against the wishes of her parents. The girl had never been found. Bulstrode and the widow planned to marry but she refused until she had made a final search for her daughter. The daughter was found but the information was never revealed to Mrs. Dunkirk. The only persons who shared the secret were Bulstrode and Mr. Raffles who was paid for keeping silent and remaining out or sight. Bulstrode married the widow Dunkirk and, subsequently, became heir to all of her wealth when she died five years later.

COMMENT: We are able to deduce that Mrs. Dunkirk's lost daughter was the mother of Will Ladislaw. He, therefore, is the proper heir to the Dunkirk fortune.

Bulstrode goes to visit Will and reveals their connection. In order to prevent a scandal, he offers Will five hundred pounds a year and a share in his own estate after his death. Will speaks scornfully to Bulstrode. He tells him he wants no part of any money that was made dishonestly.

BOOK SIX, CHAPTER SIXTY-TWO

After leaving Bulstrode, Will plans to pay a final visit to Dorothea and then to leave Middlemarch. He writes her a note but she is not at home when it arrives. Sir James, because of his hatred for Will, has been spreading rumors of the friendship between Will and Rosamond Lydgate. Dorothea defends Will against the gossip but, when she accidently meets him at Tipton Grange and discovers that he is leaving for good, she wonders if he fears possible involvement with Rosamond. Dorothea fails to realize that it is because of her alone that he has made his choice. Will's final words, however, reassure her that he loves her truly. He leaves Middlemarch the following evening.

BOOK SEVEN; TWO TEMPTATIONS, CHAPTER SIXTY-THREE

Some of the townspeople, especially Rev. Farebrother, are aware that Lydgate is in financial difficulty. Lydgate prefers to keep his problems to himself; confiding in no one and asking assistance from no one (although Farebrother would be able to help him if he asked). It occurs to no one that Lydgate's marriage to Rosamond is not completely happy: she is becoming less attentive to her husband and to the problems she is creating for him.

BOOK SEVEN, CHAPTER SIXTY-FOUR

Finally Lydgate realizes that he must make a last plea to Rosamond to be more economical in her way of life. Spoiled and childish, she begins to cry and refuses to change anything. In fact, she accuses him of stinginess. Her only suggestions are that they leave Middlemarch so that he can find a better paying position; they can also seek the help of his uncle, Sir Godwin. He tells her that he has planned to rent their house so that they will have more money. Stubbornly refusing to do as he wishes, she writes to Lydgate's uncle for help and also writes to the renting agent advising that they have changed their plans about renting the house. She tells Lydgate of neither of these letters.

Lydgate's discovery of what she has done fills him with anger and despair; yet he realizes that she will not change; eventually he must ask his uncle, Sir Godwin, for help.

BOOK SEVEN, CHAPTER SIXTY-FIVE

One morning, a letter comes in the mail addressed to Dr. Tertius Lydgate. Rosamond notices that it is from Sir Godwin. Lydgate opens and reads the letter from his uncle who reveals to him that he is "not likely to have cash to spare." Angrily, Lydgate accuses Rosamond of meddling; she accuses him of mistreating her saying it is she who has been wronged. Because he is kind-hearted and loves her, Lydgate forgives her again, and even apologizes for his behavior. He tells her he realizes their situation is "ten times harder for her than for him."

BOOK SEVEN, CHAPTER SIXTY-SIX

Lydgate must now think of some means to raise money to pay his debts. Thinking of selling his horse and buying a cheaper one, he goes into the Green Dragon to speak to Mr. Bambridge, the horse dealer. While there, he meets Fred Vincy; he appears to be falling back to his bad habits although he is still working with Caleb Garth as his assistant. Rev. Farebrother, noticing Fred's failings, cautions him that, if he is ever to win Mary's respect and love, he must work harder to prove himself.

BOOK SEVEN, CHAPTER SIXTY-SEVEN

Since Sir Godwin has refused to assist Lydgate in his financial difficulties, the doctor unwillingly comes to the conclusion that there is no one for him to turn to but Mr. Bulstrode. He hesitates because of his dislike for Bulstrode. He receives a note from the banker stating that he wants to consult Lydgate at the Bank about his "complaints": (Lydgate has a tendency towards hypochondria).

He plans to use this opportunity to ask for the loan. Bulstrode is unsympathetic (because of his own problems with Raffles). He advises Lydgate to declare himself in the state of bankruptcy. The banker then tells the doctor that he has been considering leaving Middlemarch and transferring the management of the hospital to Dorothea. She is now a wealthy woman.

> **COMMENT:** Bulstrode hopes that, by leaving Middlemarch, he will avoid any scandal about his past if Mr. Raffles should decide to talk.

BOOK SEVEN, CHAPTER SIXTY-EIGHT

On Christmas Eve, Raffles again visits Bulstrode who has told his wife that he is "simply taking care of this wretched creature, the victim of vice, who might otherwise injure himself." He calls for a carriage for Raffles and warns him that he will pay him money only if he remains away from Middlemarch. If he returns, there will be no money for him.

Despite this arrangement with Raffles, Bulstrode senses that the only sure way for him to avoid a scandal is to leave Middlemarch. He asks the manager of his estate, Caleb Garth, to find a tenant for his house at Stone Court. Mr. Garth's first thought for manager of the property is Fred Vincy.

> **COMMENT**: We can see that Mr. Garth's deeper purpose in asking Bulstrode to appoint Fred as manager at Stone Court lies in the hope that a responsible position will make Fred a responsible person; one whom his daughter could be permitted to marry.

BOOK SEVEN, CHAPTER SIXTY-NINE

Caleb Garth ruhes into the Bank where Lydgate is speaking to Mr. Bulstrode to tell him that he has found a man lying in the road whose name is Raffles; he is gravely ill and is calling for a doctor. Bulstrode is stunned; Caleb then reveals to him that he also knows of Bulstrode's past because Raffles told him as he lay in the road. Quickly, Caleb offers to resign from his position as manager of Bulstrode's estate.

Lydgate arrives to examine Raffles and diagnoses his ailment as alcohol poisoning. He prescribes medicine and advises Bulstrode (who had speedily returned to Stone Court before the arrival of Lydgate) that Raffles is to have no more alcohol or opium.

As Lydgate returns home to his own problems, he sees his creditors removing some of his furniture because he has not been able to pay for it. Rosamond is noticeably shaken.

BOOK SEVEN, CHAPTER SEVENTY

Bulstrode is determined to keep a constant watch over Raffles so that no one other than Caleb Garth will learn his story. He begins to think that, perhaps, he was hasty in his refusal of a loan to Lydgate. The doctor pays a visit to Raffles and prescribes extremely moderate doses of opium in case of sleeplessness. Before he leaves, Bulstrode presents him with a check for one thousand pounds.

At six o'clock that evening, Bulstrode begins administering small doses of opium to the restless Raffles. Later in the night, he turns Raffles' care over to Mrs. Abel, his housekeeper. He forgets to tell her when the medication should stop.

Raffles dies the next morning but no one questions the circumstances about his death.

COMMENT: The question of guilt is presented in the chapter. Bulstrode is clearly responsible for Raffles' death.

BOOK SEVEN, CHAPTER SEVENTY-ONE

Before his death, Raffles was in the Green Dragon Tavern and Mr. Bambridge heard him bragging to those present of the hold he had over the banker, Mr. Bulstrode. He and his friend, Frank Howley, begin to talk of Lydgate's presence at Raffles' bedside before his death. They note that the doctor has been able to pay off his debts within five days of Raffles' funeral. They feel it is necessary to "put two and two together." Before long, rumors have spread throughout the town regarding the suspicions surrounding the death. Caleb Garth comes to Bulstrode to tell him that he must seek other employment; he cannot be happy working for Bulstrode. The banker receives another shock at a town meeting: In the presence of all, Frank Hawley demands that Bulstrode reveal everything in order to clear himself. Shaken by the day's events, Bulstrode is assisted home by Lydgate who begins to think that something foul may have happened. He fears that he may appear to be involved because of the money he has received from Bulstrode.

BOOK EIGHT: SUNSET AND SUNRISE, CHAPTER SEVENTY-TWO

All of the townspeople who know Lydgate are anxious to prove his innocence in the matter of Raffles' death. However, the circumstances surrounding the death leave them somewhat confused and suspicious. Dorothea is firmly convinced of his innocence but she does not wish to confront him directly about the matter. Since Bulstrode has transferred the management of the New Hospital to her and she does have certain questions to ask Lydgate about it, she sees an opportunity to question him indirectly about Raffles' death.

BOOK EIGHT, CHAPTER SEVENTY-THREE

Lydgate himself is ready "to curse the day" he came to Middlemarch. His marriage is not the success he had hoped for; now, his reputation is at stake because of Raffles and Bulstrode. He wants to clear himself but does not wish to implicate Bulstrode; especially if he is innocent because he is, now, indebted to Bulstrode for the thousand pounds Bulstrode gave him the night before Raffles' death. Yet, he tells Rosamond nothing.

BOOK EIGHT, CHAPTER SEVENTY-FOUR

Because Middlemarch is a small town, it is not long before Rosamond and Mrs. Bulstrode hear the stories about their husbands. Mrs. Bulstrode is deeply perturbed; especially since she still believes the story Bulstrode told her about Raffles being a sick, helpless man whom he had befriended. She can obtain no information from Lydgate so she finally confronts Mr. Bulstrode. Both begin to cry; his confession is silent. She cannot say, "How much is only slander and false suspicion?" and he cannot say, "I am innocent."

BOOK EIGHT, CHAPTER SEVENTY-FIVE

Rosamond, however, is completely involved with her own wishes and the gratification of them. She remains unchanged; she is grateful that their debts have been paid but she cannot feel any happier about the success of her marriage.

She first learns of the story about Raffles on a visit to her family. When Lydgate finds her silent and cold towards him, he realizes she must have heard the rumors. She cannot sympathize or console him with his problems because of her selfishness. Her only wish is that Will Ladislaw will return from London so she can tell him of her difficult life with Tertius Lydgate.

BOOK EIGHT, CHAPTER SEVENTY-SIX

Dorothea questions Lydgate about the management of the New Hospital. He mentions that he has been thinking of leaving Middlemarch. She takes this opportunity to beg him to tell her the truth of the Raffles matter and, at the same time, she proclaims his innocence. Dorothea believes his story; telling him that she will do all within her power to clear his name. She even offers to repay his loan from Bulstrode.

Lydgate hopes he will be able to convince Rosamond that he wishes to stay in Middlemarch at least until the townspeople believe his innocence in the matter.

BOOK EIGHT, CHAPTER SEVENTY-SEVEN

The following day, Dorothea pays a visit to Rosamond to explain her plans about using her money to clear Lydgate's name of scandal. She enters the drawing-room; seated with his back toward her, speaking in a low voice to Rosamond is Will Ladislaw. Seeing Dorothea, his eyes seem "to turn to marble." Although shaken, Dorothea says (in a firm voice) that she has come to leave a letter for Dr. Lydgate. This turns out to be the note for one thousand pounds for Bulstrode. Indignant after her expedition, she returns to Freshitt Hall; where she is still living with Celia and Sir James.

BOOK EIGHT, CHAPTER SEVENTY-EIGHT

Rosamond and Will stand almost paralyzed with shock from their experience, Will flies into a rage; Rosamond is in misery. He leaves feeling that any hope of a future with Dorothea is ruined. Rosamond, still concerned with her own feelings, retires to bed. Lydgate finds her there in a hysterical condition when he returns home. He knows that Dorothea went to visit his wife that afternoon but he has no idea of what happened or that Dorothea never spoke to Rosamond.

BOOK EIGHT, CHAPTER SEVENTY-NINE

Lydgate does not ask Rosamond if Dorothea has called to visit but, when he sees her letter on the table in the drawing-room, he knows she was there. Will Ladislaw arrives; Lydgate tells him that Rosamond is ill but he does not know that Will had visited earlier that day. The topic of their conversation is the one most discussed in Middlemarch; Raffles' death. Will admits only that he has had an encounter with Raffles but he makes no mention of Burlstrode's connection with him. When Lydgate tells Will that Dorothea is the only one who has come to his assistance, he notices a change in Will's face and, suddenly, he realizes that Dorothea is the reason for Will's return to Middlemarch. "The two men were pitying each other," but both were very much interested in their own problems.

BOOK EIGHT, CHAPTER EIGHTY

That evening, Dorothea dines with Rev. Farebrother and his family. She is glad to have something to do to take her mind off Will. When Will's name is brought up, in conversation, the anguish returns to Dorothea and she soon excuses herself. At home, she cries herself to sleep.

The next morning, she resolves again to be clear-headed by attempting a second visit to the troubled Lydgate household to speak to Rosamond.

BOOK EIGHT, CHAPTER EIGHTY-ONE

At the time of Dorothea's second visit, Lydgate is home with Rosamond. He fails to undestand the reason for a second call. Rosamond is in her dressing-room and is startled to hear of Dorothea's presence. She explains to Rosamond that she had come the previous day to tell her of her plans to clear Lydgate's name. Rosamond, amazed to see that Dorothea is so sincere, begins to cry with shame. When Dorothea mentions Rosamond's relationship to Will, Rosamond quickly tells her that she is mistaken about what she had seen the previous day; that Will had told her of his love for another woman.

> **COMMENT:** After Dorothea leaves, Rosamond realizes that she must be more considerate of her husband and less concerned with her own feelings. Dorothea now realizes that it is she whom Will loves; he had been telling the selfish Rosamond that he could have no feeling for her. Dorothea misunderstood the situation when she called the previous day.

BOOK EIGHT, CHAPTER EIGHTY-TWO

Will thinks he has no choice now but to leave Middlemarch again. His primary reason for returning had been to see Dorothea; now, he feels that she will have nothing to do with him.

On a visit to the Lydgate household, Rosamond tells him that she has explained the situation to Dorothea. Exhilerated at this news, Will hopes for a reconciliation with Dorothea.

BOOK EIGHT, CHAPTER EIGHTY-THREE

Dorothea is relieved after her conversation with Rosamond. On the second morning after her visit, Miss Henrietta Noble, aunt of Rev. Farebrother, pays a visit to her at the request of Will Ladislaw. She says he fears he has offended her and asks if he may see her for a few minutes. Dorothea agrees. When he comes, she tells him she is "glad" he came. They stand silently at first but finally they confess their love for one another. He tells her that he cannot marry her because of Casaubon's will by which she will lose the remaining money if they marry. She tells him she hates her wealth and her heart will break if he leaves. They decide to marry within three weeks.

BOOK EIGHT, CHAPTER EIGHTY-FOUR

Mr. Brook is the first person to tell Celia and Sir James of Dorothea's forthcoming marriage to Will. Sir James turns "white with rage" and calls it "perfectly scandalous." Celia visits Dorothea to persuade her to change her mind but she will not listen to her sister. She tells her that nothing can change her resolve.

COMMENT: Sir James is enraged over Dorothea's second marriage primarily because he sees it only as a loss of the fortune left to her in Rev. Casaubon's will. He ignores her happiness.

BOOK EIGHT, CHAPTER EIGHTY-FIVE

Bulstrode still has not made a full confession of his past life to his wife. He decides that some day (when he is dying) he will "tell her all." Mrs. Bulstrode suggests that they make amends to the Lydgates who are also leaving Middlemarch. Bulstrode knows, however, that the doctor would not accept anything from him. Mrs. Bulstrode also advises him to make Fred Vincy the manager of the property at Stone Court. (Caleb Garth had resigned after Raffles told him of Mr. Bulstrode's past life.)

BOOK EIGHT, CHAPTER EIGHTY-SIX

Caleb Garth learns of Mr. Bulstrode's plan to make Fred Vincy the manager of Stone Court. He wants to be the first to tell his daughter, Mary. She is sitting in the garden. He casually begins a conversation about Fred; although she admits her love for him, she observes "we must wait for each other a long while." When he tells her the news, she is filled with joy and rushes to tell Fred who is coming to the garden to visit her. Fred is surprised and delighted. He and Mary sit in the garden for a long time to discuss their future.

FINALE

Mary and Fred Garth had both a happy and successful marriage. He became a theoretic and practical farmer and won the admiration of the people of Middlemarch. They had three sons to bless their marriage.

Dr. Lydgate gained an excellent practice in the area surrounding London. He and Rosamond "adjusted" to one another; accepting the good and bad points of each. He was a successful man but he died at fifty leaving Rosamond and their four children. Later, she married and elderly and wealthy physician.

Dorothea and Will were still bound together by their strong love. She never repented that she had given up her wealth for marriage to Will. He continued to work for the reforms which he had begun when he was a youth.

Mr. Brooke continued to correspond with Dorothea and, when they had a son, he told Celia and Sir James (who had never forgiven Dorothea's marriage to Will) that he wished to see his new nephew before he died. The visit prompted a reconciliation between the two families and they visited each other after that.

Those who did not know Dorothea usually thought she could not have been "a nice woman" because she married a much older man and, a year after his death, married a man young enough to be her first husband's son. Dorothea, however, lead an important if obscure life; her good acts had a diffusive effect upon those around her. "The growing of good in the world is partly dependent on unhistoric acts." Our life is not as bad for us as it might have been owing to the number of people like Dorothea who led hidden lives and who rest in "unvisited tombs."

CHIEF CHARACTERS IN MIDDLEMARCH

Dorothea Brooke (later Mrs. Casaubon, Mrs. Ladislaw): The idealistic and intelligent "heroine" of the novel.

Miss Celia Brooke: Her younger sister. Less intense than Dorothea, she marries Sir James Chettam who had originally courted her sister Dorothea.

Mr. Arthur Brooke: The uncle of Dorothea and Celia. He represents a kind of sturdy English squire.

Rev. Edward Casaubon: A pedantic man. He marries Dorothea because he sees in her a companion and secretary.

Will Ladislaw: The young, handsome relative of Mr. Casaubon whose artistic and literary skills make him suspect to the people of Middlemarch. He becomes editor of the town newspaper, *Pioneer.*

Dr. Tertius Lydgate: The "hero" of the novel is a medical man whose ideals and visionary plans are dimmed by the reality of a marriage to the selfish Rosamond Vincy.

Fred Vincy: Rosamond's young, careless brother whose debts and lack of purpose prevent him from marrying his love, Mary Garth.

Nicholas Bulstrode: A strong, influential banker who suddenly discovers that his past life may be revealed and his reputation in Middlemarch destroyed.

John Raffles: The coarse, unscrupulous blackmailer who uses his knowledge of Will Ladislaw's and Mr. Burlstrode's pasts to make money.

Joshua Rigg: The "frog-faced" man who becomes the heir to the land and fortune of Peter Featherstone, since he is his natural son.

Rosamond: The beautiful but self-centered daughtetr of the mayor of Middlemarch; the debutante who becomes the wife of Dr. Lydgate.

Mary Garth: The plain and practical daughter of the estate agent, Caleb Garth, who insists that her fiance, Fred Vincy, prove his ability before their marriage.

ESSAY QUESTIONS AND ANSWERS

1. Who are the major characters in *Middlemarch* and what do they represent?

ANSWER: The major emphasis in this extensive gallery of English life is found in the portraits of two idealistic people: Dorothea Brooke (Mrs. Casaubon) and Dr. Tertius Lydgate. Both are intelligent, scrupulous and dedicated to the task of improving the lot of their fellowmen. He wishes to succeed in a far-reaching experiment and to broaden the effectiveness of the country hospital. She is concerned with improving the living conditions of poorer working classes by advocating the construction of modest cottages. Both visionaries, however, quickly find that ideas and ideals are, in themselves, no assurance of success. The way of the world is strong; complex obstacles appear to obstruck the best intentioned plans. Human avarice, pettiness, or plain preverseness block human progress. Perhaps, the chief concern of the novel is to present two thoughtful, sensitive people who are forced continually to sustain their strength in realities of living.

2. Why is Middlemarch considered one of George Eliot's best novels?

ANSWER: The book is highly representative of the most significant contributions which George Eliot has made in English literature and in the development of the novel. First, it presents a vivid and accurate panorama of English life in the third decade of the nineteenth century. Readers, such as William Wordsworth, agreed that the pictures of rural people were authentic; from the wealthier class of squires and managers, down through the middle-class pictures of clergymen and professionals, to the simple farmers and journeymen, there is an unmistakable truth in her description and psychology. Secondly, the complexity of the plot interests the reader consistently; skillful suspension of decision, which many characters face, stimulates curiosity; the abrupt revelation of sudden or hidden incidents creates surprise and intensifies interest. Thirdly, a mastery of deftness in characterization makes the reader interested in the future of most of the characters. Rarely are we unable to percieve a distinct human being made unique through specific details of speech, outlook, or action. Eliot's gifted insight into human motivation is apparent throughout; the characters act according to their natures after consideration of their choices. The effective use of dialogue, suggestive imagery, autobiographical, ethical and technical considerations also contribute to make *Middlemarch* a most valuable and artistic novel.

CRITICAL COMMENTARY

The attitude of many critics in the twentieth century about Victorian literature has been a mixture of indifference and contempt because of the marked impact of Freudian and Jungian psychological theory, the watersheds of two world wars and the influence of Marxist and Zolan philosophy. Yet for those who actually read the works of Dickens, Thackeray, and their contemporaries the experience is rewarding. Apart from other considerations these novelists and, in particular, George Eliot were accomplished storytellers. Narrative, even in the stream-of-consciousness technique, involves incident; the mode and quality of the aciton creates the interest, suspense and surprise which characterize successful fiction. And here, in story plot, is precisely where one finds the key to success in Eliot's novels. As Lord David Cecil has observed *in Early Victorian Novelists*: "It is very rore for a Victorian novelist before George Eliot to conceive the story as an organic whole of which every incident and character forms a contributory and integral part." A juxtaposition of the double plots in *Silas Marner* (see chart) fails to suggest the elaborate planning of incident effectively concealing the "coincidence" necessary to unite the separate plot strands. The realistic quality of major incidents places no excessive burden upon the reader's credulity. Since what happens is probable—as when Molly Farren, on her way to the Red House, succumbs to her final drugged sleep at Silas' door—we accept it willingly. Our suspension of disbelief is not impaired since the motives and events which are presented to us in the action are justifiable and logical within the story's realm.

Although George Eliot's technical skill is, perhaps, related chiefly to structural aspects, understanding and unravelling basic motivations found in human action is vital to her work. Claude Bisell (*A Journal of English Literary History XVIII*) suggests "George Eliot is at her strongest and best working in a social setting that she thoroughly understands and exploring a complicated network of motives with assurance and precision." The tracing of the thought of a character before he acts is a favorite interest of Eliot. The elaborate thought labyrinths of Henry James' characters are found only in Eliot's "aristocratic" characters (of which there are relatively few in her novels). She is most accomplished, however, in explication of the thinking of the types that she understood best: the sturdy, respectable middle-class and less complex lower-classes of the era in which she lived. Years of extended observation and real experience in Warwickshire and Coventry with the kind of people shown in her novels is reflected continually. Her preference is for unobtrusive picturing of the details of a character's thinking. Her use of the dramatic is very sparing and effective, as when it is employed in the opening conflict scene between Godfrey and Dunsey

Cass, or in the renunciation scene with Eppie, Silas, Nancy, and Godfrey.

Discussing the need for the dramatic in *The Craft of Fiction,* Percy Lubbock has noted: "Inevitably as the plot thickens and the climax approaches—inevitably, whenever an impression is to be emphasized and driven home—narration gives place to enactment . . . Most novelists, I think, seem to betray, like Thackeray, a preference for one method or the other, for picture or for drama; one sees in a moment how Fielding, Balzac, George Eliot, incline to the first, in their diverse manners, and Tolstoy (certainly Tolstoy, in spite of his big range) or Dostoevsky to the second, the scenic way."

That Eliot may have been influenced in her style by Balzac is perhaps a valid observation since in an essay which appeared in *The Leader,* July 21, 1855 "The Morality of Wilhelm Meister" she eulogized Balzac as "perhaps the most wonderful writer of fiction the world has ever seen." That she could hardly have permitted herself to imitate his naturalism, however, is forcefully underlined by her comment in the same article "he drags us by his magic force through scene after scene of unmitigated vice, till the effect of walking among the human carrion is a moral nausea."

From the English critic F. R. Leavis *The Great Tradition* (London, 1948, pp. 124-25) comes the strong statement of Eliot superiority over the later Victorian novelists and a comparison of Eliot with Leo Tolstoy, the author of **War and Peace:** "I affirm my conviction that, by the side of George Eliot—and the comparison shouldn't be necessary —Meredith appears as a shallow exhibitionist . . . and Hardy, decent as he is, as a provincial manufacturer of gauche and heavy fictions that sometimes have corresponding value. For a positive indication of her place and quality I think of a Russian, not Turgenev, but a far greater, Tolstoy—who, we all know, is pre-eminent in getting the 'spirit of life itself'. George Eliot, of course, is not as transcendentally great as Tolstoy, but she *is* great, and great in the same way . . . Of George Eliot it can be said that her best work has a Tolstoyan depth and reality."

Because of the advances made in fiction techniques and scientific knowledge of the human psyche the twentieth century novelist has at his disposal much direction which George Eliot did not receive. Although their hasty and dilletante tastes prevent many readers and critics from even reading her novels, (one supposes because of the appended didacticism of occasional chapters and a mistaken view that stereotyped sentimentality drips from every page), the real nature of her style and value remains unknown.

Eliot's brilliant psychological penetration was one of the English models for which Proust admitted great admiration. The quality novels of

Woolf, Joyce and Faulkner and a handful of European novelists represent the best, in terms of technical advances and plumbing of the mind, that the twentieth century has produced. For her time, George Eliot's contribution both for virtuosity in form and in psychological depth were unmatched.

SUGGESTED BIBLIOGRAPHY

The complete *Works* of George Eliot has been published in twenty-five volumes (Warwickshire edition, 1908). Following is a list of titles under two general topics. Plentiful material concerning *Silas Marner* and *Middlemarch* may be found in the works listed.

LETTERS

Haight, G. S. (ed.) *The George Eliot Letters.* 7 vols.

BIOGRAPHY

Cross, J. W. *George Eliot's Life as Related in her Letters and Journals.* 3 vols. (1885)
Hanson, L. and E. M. *Marian Evans and George Eliot.* (1952)
Stevens, George. *George Eliot.* (1902)
Haldane, E. S. *George Eliot and her Times.* (1927)
May, J. Lewis. *George Eliot; a Study.* (1930)
Bullett, Gerald. *George Eliot: Her Life and Books.* (1947)
Williams, Blanche C. *George Eliot: A Biography.* (1936)

CRITICISM

Thale, Jerome. *The Novels of George Eliot.* (1959)
Stump, Reva. *Movement and Vision in George Eliot's Novels.* (1959)
Bennett, Joan. *George Eliot: Her Mind and Art.* (1948)

INDIVIDUAL CHAPTERS OF CRITICISM

Woolf, Virginia. *The Common Reader.* (1925)
Cecil, Lord David. *Early Victorian Novelists.* (1935)
Leavis, F. R. *The Great Tradition.* (1948)
Baugh, Albert C. and others. *A Literary History of England.* (1948)
Stevenson, Lionel. *The English Novel.* (1960)
Baker, Ernest. *The English Novel.* Vols. III, IV. (1930, 1934)

NOTES